Advance pra.

THE METAMORPHOSIS

"This fine version, with David Cronenberg's inspired introduction and the new translator's beguiling afterword, is, I suspect, the most disturbing though the most comforting of all so far; others will follow, but don't hesitate: this is the transforming text for you."

—Richard Howard

"A classic, magisterial work of fiction has been dusted off and wondrously restored to its freshness and originality by one of our best contemporary translators. Susan Bernofsky is alive to the humor, irony, and sheer mischief behind Kafka's prose. David Cronenberg's shrewd, sympathetic introduction adds just the right grace note."

—Phillip Lopate

"Susan Bernofsky brilliantly infuses her splendid and (deceptively) comfortable prose with the dark ambience of the old world, giving rise to the grim and unabashed hilarity that is *Metamorphosis*. Bernofsky's translation of Kafka's morbid comedy is fiendishly funny, fresh and necessary."   —Binnie Kirshenbaum,
author of *Hester Among the Ruins*

"An ideally uneasy triumph of a translation."

—Rivka Galchen

THE METAMORPHOSIS

W. W. NORTON & COMPANY

New York • *London*

FRANZ KAFKA

THE

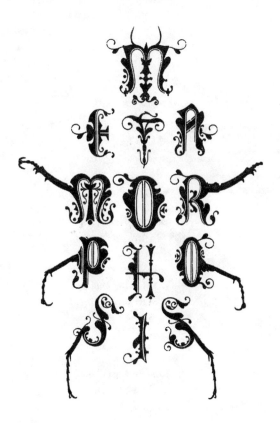

METAMORPHOSIS

A NEW TRANSLATION BY SUSAN BERNOFSKY

For information about permission to reproduce selections from this book,
write to Permissions, W. W. Norton & Company, Inc.,
500 Fifth Avenue, New York, NY 10110

For information about special discounts for bulk purchases,
please contact W. W. Norton Special Sales
at specialsales@wwnorton.com or 800-233-4830

Manufacturing by LSC Communications, Harrisonburg
Book design by Chris Welch
Production manager: Louise Mattarelliano

Library of Congress Cataloging-in-Publication Data

Kafka, Franz, 1883–1924.
[Verwandlung. English]
The metamorphosis / Franz Kafka ; a new translation by Susan Bernofsky. —
First edition.
pages cm
ISBN 978-0-393-34709-8 (pbk.)
I. Bernofsky, Susan, translator. II. Title.
PT2621.A26V413 2014
833'.912—dc23
2013033145

W. W. Norton & Company, Inc.
500 Fifth Avenue, New York, N.Y. 10110
www.wwnorton.com

W. W. Norton & Company Ltd.
15 Carlisle Street, London W1D 3BS

CONTENTS

INTRODUCTION
THE BEETLE AND THE FLY

David Cronenberg

I woke up one morning recently to discover that I was a seventy-year-old man. Is this different from what happens to Gregor Samsa in *The Metamorphosis*? He wakes up to find that he's become a near-human-sized beetle (probably of the scarab family, if his household's charwoman is to be believed), and not a particularly robust specimen at that. Our reactions, mine and Gregor's, are very similar. We are confused and bemused, and think that it's a momentary delusion that will soon dissipate, leaving our lives to continue as they were. What could the source of these twin transformations possibly be? Certainly, you can see a birthday coming from many miles away, and it should not be a shock or a surprise when it happens. And as any well-meaning friend will tell you, seventy is just a number. What impact can that number really have on an actual, unique physical human life?

In the case of Gregor, a young traveling salesman spending a night at home in his family's apartment in Prague, awakening into a strange, human/insect hybrid existence is, to say the obvious, a surprise he did not see coming, and the reaction of his household—mother, father, sister, maid, cook—is to recoil in benumbed horror, as one would expect, and not one member of his family feels compelled to console the creature by, for example, pointing out that a beetle is also a living thing, and turning into one might, for a mediocre human living a humdrum life, be an exhilarating and elevating experience, and so what's the problem? This imagined consolation could not, in any case, take place within the structure of the story, because Gregor can understand human speech, but cannot be understood when he tries to speak, and so his family never think to approach him as a creature with human intelligence. (It must be noted, though, that in their bourgeois banality, they somehow accept that this creature is, in some unnamable way, their Gregor. It never occurs to them that, for example, a giant beetle has eaten Gregor; they don't have the imagination, and he very quickly becomes not much more than a housekeeping problem.) His transformation seals him within himself as surely as if he had suffered a total paralysis. These two scenarios, mine and Gregor's, seem so different, one might ask why I even bother to compare them. The source of the transformations is the same, I argue: we have both awakened to a forced awareness of what we really are, and that awareness is profound and irreversible; in each case, the delusion soon proves to be a new, mandatory reality, and life does not continue as it did.

Is Gregor's transformation a death sentence or, in some way, a fatal diagnosis? Why does the beetle Gregor not survive? Is it his human brain, depressed and sad and melancholy, that betrays the insect's basic sturdiness? Is it the brain that defeats the bug's urge to survive, even to eat? What's wrong with that beetle? Beetles, the order of insect called *Coleoptera*, which means "sheathed wing" (though Gregor never seems to discover his own wings, which are presumably hiding under his hard wing casings), are notably hardy and well adapted for survival; there are more species of beetle than any other order on earth. Well, we learn that Gregor has bad lungs— they are "none too reliable"—and so the Gregor beetle has bad lungs as well, or at least the insect equivalent, and perhaps that really is his fatal diagnosis; or perhaps it's his growing inability to eat that kills him, as it did Kafka, who ultimately coughed up blood and died of starvation caused by laryngeal tuberculosis at the age of forty. What about me? Is my seventieth birthday a death sentence? Of course, yes, it is, and in some ways it has sealed me within myself as surely as if I had suffered a total paralysis. And this revelation is the function of the bed, and of dreaming in the bed, the mortar in which the minutiae of everyday life are crushed, ground up, and mixed with memory and desire and dread. Gregor awakes from troubled dreams which are never directly described by Kafka. Did Gregor dream that he was an insect, then awake to find that he was one? "'What in the world has happened to me?' he thought." "It was no dream," says Kafka, referring to Gregor's new physical form, but it's not clear that his troubled dreams were anticipatory insect dreams. In the movie I co-wrote and directed of George Langelaan's short story *The Fly*,

I have our hero Seth Brundle, played by Jeff Goldblum, say, while deep in the throes of his transformation into a hideous fly/human hybrid, "I'm an insect who dreamt he was a man and loved it. But now the dream is over, and the insect is awake." He is warning his former lover that he is now a danger to her, a creature with no compassion and no empathy. He has shed his humanity like the shell of a cicada nymph, and what has emerged is no longer human. He is also suggesting that to be a human, a self-aware consciousness, is a dream that cannot last, an illusion. Gregor too has trouble clinging to what is left of his humanity, and as his family begins to feel that this thing in Gregor's room is no longer Gregor, he begins to feel the same way. But unlike Brundle's fly self, Gregor's beetle is no threat to anyone but himself, and starves and fades away like an afterthought as his family revels in their freedom from the shameful, embarrassing burden that he has become.

When *The Fly* was released in 1986, there was much conjecture that the disease that Brundle had brought on himself was a metaphor for AIDS. Certainly I understood this—AIDS was on everybody's mind as the vast scope of the disease was gradually being revealed. But for me, Brundle's disease was more fundamental: in an artificially accelerated manner, he was aging. He was a consciousness that was aware that it was a body that was mortal, and with acute awareness and humor participated in that inevitable transformation that all of us face, if only we live long enough. Unlike the passive and helpful but anonymous Gregor, Brundle was a star in the firmament of science, and it was a bold and reckless experiment in transmitting matter through space (his DNA mixes with that of an errant fly) that caused his predicament.

Langelaan's story, first published in *Playboy* magazine in 1957, falls firmly within the genre of science fiction, with all the mechanics and reasonings of its scientist hero carefully, if fancifully, constructed (two used telephone booths are involved). Kafka's story, of course, is not science fiction; it does not provoke discussion regarding technology and the hubris of scientific investigation, or the use of scientific research for military purposes. Without sci-fi trappings of any kind, *The Metamorphosis* forces us to think in terms of analogy, of reflexive interpretation, though it is revealing that none of the characters in the story, including Gregor, ever does think that way. There is no meditation on a family secret or sin that might have induced such a monstrous reprisal by God or the Fates, no search for meaning even on the most basic existential plane. The bizarre event is dealt with in a perfunctory, petty, materialistic way, and it arouses the narrowest range of emotional response imaginable, almost immediately assuming the tone of an unfortunate natural family occurrence with which one must reluctantly contend.

Stories of magical transformations have always been part of humanity's narrative canon. They articulate that universal sense of empathy for all life forms that we feel; they express that desire for transcendence that every religion also expresses; they prompt us to wonder if transformation into another living creature would be a proof of the possibility of reincarnation and some sort of afterlife and is thus, however hideous or disastrous the narrative, a religious and hopeful concept. Certainly my Brundlefly goes through moments of manic strength and power, convinced that he has combined the best components of human and insect to become a super being, refusing to see his personal evolution as anything but a victory even as he begins to shed his human body parts, which he carefully stores in a medicine cabinet he calls the Brundle Museum of Natural History.

There is none of this in *The Metamorphosis*. The Samsabeetle is barely aware that he is a hybrid, though he takes small hybrid pleasures where he can find them, whether it's hanging from the ceiling or scuttling through the mess and dirt of his room (beetle pleasure) or listening to the music that his sister plays on her violin (human pleasure). But the Samsa family is the Samsabeetle's context and his cage, and his subservience to the needs of his family both before and after his transformation extends, ultimately, to his realization that it would be more convenient for them if he just disappeared, it would be an expression of his love for them, in fact, and so he does just that, by quietly dying. The Samsabeetle's short life, fantastical though it is, is played out on the level of the resolutely mundane and the functional, and fails to provoke in the story's characters any hint of philosophy, meditation, or profound reflection. How similar would the story be, then, if on that fateful morning, the Samsa family found in the room of their son not a young, vibrant traveling salesman who is supporting them by his unselfish and endless labor, but a shuffling, half-blind, barely ambulatory eighty-nine-year-old man using insectlike canes, a man who mumbles incoherently and has soiled his trousers and out of the shadowland of his dementia projects anger and induces guilt? If, when Gregor Samsa woke one morning from troubled dreams, he found himself transformed right there in his bed into a demented, disabled, demanding old man? His family is horrified but somehow recognize him as their own Gregor, albeit transformed. Eventually, though, as in the beetle variant of the story, they decide that he is no longer their Gregor, and that it would be a blessing for him to disappear.

When I went on my publicity tour for *The Fly*, I was often asked what insect I would want to be if I underwent an entomological transformation. My answers varied, depending on my mood, though I had a fondness for the dragonfly, not only for its spectacular flying but also for the novelty of its ferocious underwater nymphal stage with its deadly extendable underslung jaw; I also thought that mating in the air might be pleasant. Would that be your soul, then, this dragonfly, flying heavenward? came one response. Is that not really what you're looking for? No, not really, I said. I'd just be a simple dragonfly, and then, if I managed to avoid being eaten by a bird or a frog, I would mate, and as summer ended, I would die.

THE METAMORPHOSIS

I

HEN GREGOR SAMSA WOKE ONE MORNING from troubled dreams, he found himself transformed right there in his bed into some sort of monstrous insect. He was lying on his back—which was hard, like a carapace—and when he raised his head a little he saw his curved brown belly segmented by rigid arches atop which the blanket, already slipping, was just barely managing to cling. His many legs, pitifully thin compared to the rest of him, waved helplessly before his eyes.

"What in the world has happened to me?" he thought. It was no dream. His room, a proper human room, if admittedly rather too small, lay peacefully between the four familiar walls. Above the table, where an unpacked collection of cloth samples was arranged (Samsa was a traveling salesman), hung the picture he had recently clipped from a glossy magazine and placed in an attractive gilt frame. This picture showed a lady in a fur hat and fur boa who sat erect, holding out to the viewer a heavy fur muff in which her entire forearm had vanished.

Gregor's gaze then shifted to the window, where the bleak weather—raindrops could be heard striking the metal sill—made him feel quite melancholy. "What if I just go back to sleep for a little while and forget all this foolishness," he thought, but this proved utterly impossible, for it was his habit to sleep on his right side, and in his present state he was unable to assume this position. No matter how forcefully he thrust himself onto his side, he kept rolling back. Perhaps a hundred times he attempted it, closing his eyes so as not to have to see those struggling legs, and relented only when he began to feel a faint dull ache in his side, unlike anything he'd ever felt before.

"Good Lord," he thought, "what an exhausting pro-fession I've chosen. Day in and day out on the road. Work like this is far more unsettling than business conducted at home, and then I have the agony of trav-eling itself to contend with: worrying about train con-nections, the irregular, unpalatable meals, and human intercourse that is constantly changing, never develop-ing the least constancy or warmth. Devil take it all!" He felt a faint itch high up on his belly; still on his back, he laboriously edged himself over to the bedpost so he could raise his head more easily; identified the site of the itch: a cluster of tiny white dots he was unable to judge; and wanted to probe the spot with a leg, but drew it back again at once, for the touch sent cold shiv-ers rippling through him.

He slid back into his earlier position. "All this early rising," he thought, "it's enough to make one soft in the head. Human beings need their sleep. Other traveling salesmen live like harem girls. When I go back to the boardinghouse, for example, to copy out the morning's commissions: why, these gentlemen may still be sitting at breakfast. I'd like to see my boss's face if I tried that some time; he'd can me on the spot. Although who knows, maybe that would be the best thing for me. If

I didn't have to hold back for my parents' sake, I'd have given notice long ago—I'd have marched right up to him and given him a piece of my mind. He'd have fallen right off his desk! And what an odd custom that is: perching high up atop one's elevated desk and from this considerable height addressing one's employee down below, especially as the latter is obliged to stand quite close because his boss is hard of hearing. Well, all hope is not yet lost; as soon as I've saved up enough money to pay back what my parents owe him—another five or six years ought to be enough—I'll most definitely do just that. This will be the great parting of ways. For the time being, though, I've got to get up, my train leaves at five."

And he glanced over at the alarm clock ticking away atop the wardrobe. "Heavenly Father!" he thought. It was half past six, and the clock's hands kept shifting calmly forward, in fact the half-hour had already passed, it was getting on toward six forty-five. Could the alarm have failed to ring? Even from the bed one could see it was properly set for four o'clock; it must have rung. Yes, but was it possible to sleep tranquilly through this furniture-shaking racket? Well, his sleep hadn't been exactly tranquil, but no doubt that's why it had been so sound. But what should he do now? The next train was at seven o'clock; to catch it, he would have to rush like a madman, and his sample case wasn't even packed yet, and he himself felt far from agile or alert. And even if he managed to catch this train, his boss was certain to unleash a thunderstorm of invective upon his head, for the clerk who met the five o'clock train had no doubt long since reported Gregor's absence. This clerk was the boss's underling, a creature devoid of backbone and wit. What if he called in sick? But that would be mortifying and also suspicious, since Gregor had never once been ill in all his five years of service. No doubt his boss would come calling with the company doctor, would reproach Gregor's parents for their son's laziness, silencing all objections by referring them to this doctor, in whose opinion there existed only healthy individuals unwilling to work. And would the doctor be so terribly wrong in this instance? Aside from a mild drowsiness that was certainly superfluous after so many hours of sleep, Gregor felt perfectly fine; in fact, he was ravenous.

While he was considering these matters with the greatest possible speed, yet still without managing to make up his mind to leave the bed (the clock was just striking a quarter to seven), a timid knock came at the door at the head of his bed. "Gregor," the voice called—it was his mother—"it's a quarter to seven. Didn't you want to catch your train?" That gentle voice! Gregor flinched when he heard his own in response: it was unmistakably his old voice, but now it had been infiltrated as if from below by a tortured peeping sound that was impossible to suppress—leaving each word intact, comprehensible, but only for an instant before so completely annihilating it as it continued to reverberate that a person could not tell for sure whether his ears were deceiving him. Gregor had meant to give a proper response explaining everything, but under the circumstances he limited himself to saying, "Yes, thank you, Mother, I'm just getting up." Because of the wooden door, the change in Gregor's voice appeared not to be noticeable from the other side, for his mother was reassured by his response and shuffled off. But their brief conversation had alerted the other family members that Gregor was unexpectedly still at home, and already his father was knocking at one of the room's side doors, softly, but with his fist: "Gregor, Gregor," he called. "What's the problem?" And after a short while he repeated his question in a deeper register: "Gregor! Gregor!" Meanwhile, at the other side door came his sister's faint lament: "Gregor? Are you unwell? Do you need anything?" "Just a second," Gregor answered in both directions at once, making an effort, by enunciating as clearly as possible and inserting long pauses between the individual words, to remove anything conspicuous from his voice. And in fact his father returned to his breakfast, but his sister whispered: "Gregor, open the door, I implore you." But Gregor had no intention of opening the door; he praised the cautious habit he had acquired while traveling of locking all his doors at night, even at home.

First he would get up calmly and undisturbed, he would get dressed and above all have breakfast, and only then would he consider his next steps, for all these supine contemplations, he suddenly realized, would yield no useful results. He recalled often having felt mild aches and pains in bed, caused perhaps by lying in an awkward position, and this pain had then proven to be a figment of his imagination the moment he got up; he was curious to see how this morning's imaginings would gradually fade. The change in his voice was nothing more than the harbinger of a proper head cold, an occupational hazard among traveling salesmen; this he doubted not in the least.

It was simple enough to rid himself of the blanket; he needed only puff himself up a bit, and it fell right off. But the rest proved difficult, not least because he was so exceedingly wide. He would have needed arms and hands to prop himself up; but instead all he had were these many little legs, variously in motion, that he was unable to control. If he tried to bend one leg, it would be the first to straighten; and when he finally succeeded in getting one leg to do his bidding, all the others went flailing about in an unnerving frenzy. "Enough of this lying about uselessly in bed," Gregor said to himself.

At first he tried to maneuver the lower part of his body out of the bed, but this lower part—which, by the way, he had not yet seen and couldn't properly imagine—proved too unwieldy; it all went so slowly; and when at last, half-mad with impatience, he thrust himself recklessly forward with all his strength, it was in the wrong direction, and he slammed against the lower bedpost; the throbbing pain he felt instructed him that for now at least the lower part of his body was perhaps the most sensitive.

So he decided to try leading instead with his upper

body and carefully twisted his head toward the edge of the bed. This was easily accomplished, and in the end, despite his width and weight, the mass of his body slowly followed the turning of his head. But once his head was dangling in midair outside the bed, he was afraid to keep shifting forward like this, since if eventually he had to let himself fall in this position, it would be practically a miracle if his head escaped injury. And right now he had to keep his wits about him at all costs, even if it meant staying where he was.

But when, sighing after redoubled efforts, he found himself lying there as before, watching his little legs engaged in their struggles, perhaps more flailingly now, and seeing no possible way to bring calm or order to this chaos, he told himself once more that he could not possibly remain lying here any longer and that the most sensible thing would be to sacrifice anything and everything as long as there remained even the slightest hope of liberating himself from the bed. Simultaneously, though, he continued to remind himself that calm consideration—indeed, the calmest consideration— was far preferable to resolutions seized on in despair. At such moments he fixed his eyes as sharply as possible on the window, but regrettably the view of the morning fog, which veiled even the far side of the narrow street, offered little by way of optimism and good spirits. "Seven o'clock already," he said to himself as the clock struck once more, "already seven and still such dense fog." And for a little while he lay there quietly, his breathing shallow, in the expectation, perhaps, that this perfect silence might possibly restore the real and ordinary state of things.

Then he said to himself: "Before it strikes a quarter past seven, I must absolutely have gotten myself completely out of bed. Besides, by then someone will have come from the office to inquire after me, as the office opens before seven." And he now set himself to rocking his body out of the bed as evenly as possible along his entire length. If he allowed himself to fall from the bed like this, his head—which he intended to lift up cleanly as he fell—would in all likelihood remain unharmed. His back seemed to be hard; surely it would sustain no damage as he fell to the rug. His greatest concern was what to do about the loud crash that would clearly result, no doubt calling forth not terror perhaps but certainly alarm behind each door. Nonetheless it would have to be ventured.

By the time Gregor was already protruding half-way out of bed—this new method was more a game than a struggle, all he had to do was keep rocking sideways a little at a time—it occurred to him how simple things would be if only someone came to his aid. Two strong individuals—he was thinking of his father and the maidservant—would suffice; all they'd have to do was slip their arms beneath his curved back to scoop him out of bed, then crouch down with their burden and wait patiently for him to flip himself over onto the floor, where he hoped those tiny legs of his would take on some meaning. But even aside from the fact that the doors were locked, should he really call for help? Despite his distress, he couldn't help smiling at the thought.

Already he'd reached the point where the vigorous rocking motion was making it almost impossible for him to keep his balance, and soon he would have to make up his mind and take the plunge, for a quarter after seven was only five minutes away—when the front doorbell rang. "It's someone from the office," he said to himself and nearly froze while his little legs went on scrabbling all the more frenetically. For a moment all was still. "They won't answer," Gregor said to himself, caught up in some deluded hope. But then of course, as always, the maid strode resolutely to the door and opened it.

Gregor needed only hear the visitor's first words of greeting to know who it was: the general manager himself. Why oh why was Gregor condemned to serve in a firm where even the most negligible falling short was enough to arouse the greatest possible suspicion? Was every last one of the firm's employees a scoundrel, was there not a single loyal, devoted soul among them who would be driven mad by pangs of conscience should he fail to make the best possible use of even just a few morning hours for his employer's benefit, such that his guilt would render him virtually incapable of rising from his bed? Would it really not have sufficed to send an apprentice to inquire—if indeed such inquiries were necessary at all—did the general manager have to come in person, and was it necessary to demonstrate to the entire innocent family that the investigation of this suspicious matter could be entrusted only to the general manager's sharp intellect? And more because of the agitation aroused in Gregor by this train of thought than because of some proper resolution on his part, he swung himself out of bed with all his might. There was a loud thud, you couldn't really call it a crash. The rug cushioned the impact a little, and since his back was more elastic than he'd thought, the resulting sound was muffled and not so obvious. But he hadn't managed to hold his head up carefully enough and had bumped it; he turned it this way and that, pressing it against the rug in his vexation and pain.

"Something just fell in there," the general manager now said in the room on the left. Gregor tried to imagine whether anything like what he was now experiencing could ever befall the general manager; the possibility must certainly be admitted. But as if brusquely dismissing the question, the manager now took a few purposeful steps in the next room, making his patent leather boots creak. From the room on the right came the whisper of Gregor's sister informing him: "Gregor, the general manager is here." "I know," Gregor murmured; but he didn't dare raise his voice high enough for his sister to hear.

"Gregor," his father now said from the room on the left, "the general manager has come to inquire why you failed to depart by the early train. We don't know what to tell him. Besides, he'd like to have a word with you in person. So please open the door. I'm sure he'll be kind enough not to take offense at the untidiness of your room." "Good morning, Herr Samsa," the general manager now cried out in a friendly tone. "He isn't well," Gregor's mother said to the general manager while his father was still having his say beside the door, "not well at all, take my word for it, sir. Why else would Gregor miss his train! The office is the only thing that boy ever thinks of. It really bothers me that he never goes out in the evening; he's been back in the city an entire week now, but he's spent every last evening at home. He just sits at the table with us, quietly reading the newspaper, or else studies the timetables. Even just doing woodworking projects seems to entertain him. He carved a little picture frame, for example, did it in two or three evenings with his fretsaw; you'll be amazed how pretty it is; it's hanging there in his room; you'll see it in a minute when Gregor opens the door. Oh, and I'm so glad you paid us a visit, sir; on our own we'd never have managed to persuade Gregor to open up; he's so stubborn; and surely he isn't well, even though he denied it this morning." "Be . . . right . . . there," Gregor said, not moving, so as not to miss a single word of their conversation. "No other explanation, madam, is conceivable to me," the general manager said. "Let us hope it is nothing grave. Though on the other hand I would note that, as businessmen— fortunately or unfortunately, as one will—we are very often obliged to suppress indispositions out of consideration for the firm." "So are you ready to let the general manager in?" Gregor's impatient father asked, knocking again at the door. "No," Gregor responded. In the left-hand room horrified silence, while in the room on the right Gregor's sister began to sob.

Why didn't his sister go to join the others? She must have just gotten out of bed and not yet begun to dress. And why was she crying? Because he wasn't getting up and opening his door to the general manager, because he was in danger of losing his position, and because his boss would then start hounding his parents once more over their ancient debt? For the time being, all such worries were assuredly unnecessary. Gregor was still here, and abandoning his family was the farthest thing from his thoughts. At the moment, to be sure, he was lying on the rug, and no one familiar with his current state would seriously expect him to let the general manager in. But surely he wouldn't be sent packing just like that because of so trivial an act of discourtesy, for which it would be simple enough to find an appropriate excuse later on. And it seemed to Gregor it would be far more sensible to just leave him in peace rather than disturbing him with all this weeping and cajoling. But the others were distressed by the uncertainty of it all; their behavior was understandable.

"Herr Samsa," the general manager now called out, raising his voice. "What has come over you? You barricade yourself in your room, you reply to queries only with yes and no, you cause your parents onerous, unnecessary worries, and you are neglecting—let me permit myself to note—your professional responsibilities in a truly unprecedented manner. I speak here in the name of your parents as well as your employer and in all seriousness must ask you for a clear and immediate explanation. I am astonished, utterly astonished. I have always known you as a calm, sensible person, and now it seems you've begun to permit yourself the most whimsical extravagances. To be sure, the boss did suggest one possible explanation for your absence this morning—it concerns the cash payments recently entrusted to your care—and truthfully, I all but gave him my word of honor that this explanation could not be correct. But confronted here with your incomprehensible obstinacy, I find myself losing any desire

I might have had to come to your defense. And your position is anything but secure. It was originally my intention to discuss all this with you in a private conversation, but since you compel me to waste my time here, I do not know why your esteemed parents should not hear of it as well. In short: your productivity of late has been highly unsatisfactory; admittedly this is not the best season for drumming up business, we do acknowledge this; but a season in which no business at all is drummed up is something that does not, and indeed may not exist, Herr Samsa."

"But sir," Gregor cried out, beside himself and forgetting all else in his agitation, "I shall open the door at once, this very instant. A slight indisposition, a fit of dizziness kept me from getting up. Even now I'm still in bed. But already I am feeling very much refreshed. Here, I'm getting up. Just a moment's patience! It's a bit more difficult than I thought. But already I'm feeling quite fine. How odd, the way such a thing can suddenly come over one. Yesterday evening I felt perfectly all right, my parents can attest to this, or rather: I did in fact feel a mild foreboding yesterday evening already. Surely it was noticeable to anyone looking at me. Why didn't I send word to the office? But we always just

assume we'll be able to overcome these illnesses without staying home. Sir! Do be gentle with my parents.
The allegations you make are unfounded, and no one
has ever mentioned anything of the sort to me. Perhaps
you haven't yet looked over the most recent commissions I sent in. In any case, I'll be back on the road in
time for the eight o'clock train; these additional hours
of rest have fortified me. Please do not allow me to
detain you any longer, sir; I shall be at the office myself
in no time; do be so good as to say I'm on my way and
give my regards to the boss."

And while Gregor was hastily blurting out all of
this, scarcely knowing what he said, he edged closer
to the wardrobe with minimal effort, no doubt thanks
to the practice he had already acquired while still in
bed, and now he did his best to haul himself upright.
Indeed, he really did want to open the door, to show
himself and speak with the general manager; he was
eager to learn what the others, who were so anxious to
see him, would say when they finally laid eyes on him.
If they recoiled in horror, Gregor could surrender all
responsibility and rest easy. But if they accepted it all
calmly, that meant he too had no reason to get himself
worked up, and if he hurried, he could still make it to

the station by eight. At first he couldn't get a grip on the wardrobe's smooth surface, but finally he gave a great heave and found himself standing upright; he no longer paid any heed to the pain in his lower body, ache as it might. Now he let himself drop against the back of a nearby chair, clinging to its edges with his little legs. And having thus attained control over himself, he fell silent, for now he could listen to the general manager.

"Did you understand a single word?" the manager was asking Gregor's parents. "Surely he isn't trying to make fools of us?" "For heaven's sake," Gregor's mother cried, already weeping, "he might be gravely ill, and here we are tormenting him. Grete! Grete!" she cried out. "Mother?" Gregor's sister called from the other side. They were communicating through Gregor's room. "You must go for the doctor at once. Gregor is ill. Quick, fetch the doctor. Did you hear him speaking just now?" "That was an animal's voice," the general manager said, speaking in noticeably subdued tones compared to the cries of Gregor's mother. "Anna! Anna!" the father shouted into the kitchen through the vestibule, clapping his hands. "Run and fetch a locksmith, hurry!" And already the two girls were racing through the vestibule, their skirts rustling (how had

Gregor's sister possibly gotten dressed so quickly?), and flung open the front door. There was no sound of the door closing again; no doubt they had left it standing open, as one sees with apartments in which a great calamity has occurred.

But Gregor was far less troubled now. Even though the others were no longer able to understand his words—though they had seemed to him clear enough, clearer than in the past, perhaps because his ear had grown accustomed to their sound—they were now convinced that things were not right with him and were prepared to offer help. The confidence and conviction with which these first arrangements had been made comforted him. He felt drawn once more into the circle of humankind and was expecting both the doctor and the locksmith—without properly differentiating between the two—to perform magnificent, astounding feats. So as to have as intelligible a voice as possible for the crucial discussions that lay ahead, he cleared his throat a little, making an effort to do this as discreetly as possible, since even this sound might differ from human throat-clearing, which he no longer trusted himself to judge. In the next room, meanwhile, all was quiet. Perhaps his parents sat whispering at the table with the general manager, or perhaps all of them were leaning against the door, listening.

Gregor slowly pushed himself over to the door using the armchair, then let go and allowed himself to fall against the door, propping himself upright—the pads of his little legs turned out to be slightly sticky—and there he rested briefly from his exertions. Then he set about turning the key in the lock using his mouth. Unfortunately it seemed he had no real teeth—so how was he supposed to grasp the key?—but his jaws turned out to be surprisingly strong; and with their help he actually succeeded in causing the key to move, paying no heed to the fact that he was no doubt injuring himself in the process, for a brown fluid ran out of his mouth and down the key, dripping onto the floor. "Listen to that," the general manager said in the next room, "he's turning the key in the lock." Gregor found these words most encouraging; but all of them should have been cheering him on, including his father and mother: "Come on, Gregor!" they should have shouted, "just keep at it, keep working on that lock!" And now, imagining all of them following his efforts with great suspense, he bit down on the key uncomprehendingly, with all the force he could muster. With each revolution of the key, he danced about the lock, holding himself upright using only his mouth and, as needed, either clinging to the key or using the entire weight of his body to press it down. The brighter sound of the lock finally springing open positively revived him. Sighing in relief, he said to himself: "I guess I didn't need the locksmith after all," and he laid his head upon the handle of the door to press it open.

But he remained hidden from view as the door swung toward him, even after it was wide open. To be seen, he had to work his way slowly around one of the wings of the double door, a delicate operation if he wanted to avoid plopping down awkwardly on his back before he'd even entered the room. He was still occupied with this difficult maneuver and had no leisure to attend to anything else when he heard the general manager utter a loud "Oh!"—it sounded like wind howling—and now he saw him too, saw how the general manager, who was standing closest to the door, pressed his hand to his open mouth, slowly retreating, as though being driven back by an invisible, steady force. Gregor's mother—who despite the general manager's presence stood with her hair still undone from the night, wildly bristling—first looked over at his father, her hands clasped, then took two steps in Gregor's direction before falling down in the midst of all her billowing skirts, her face vanishing completely where it sank to her bosom. Gregor's father clenched his fist with a hostile grimace, as if he intended to thrust Gregor back into his room, then glanced uncertainly about the living room, shaded his eyes with his hands, and wept until his mighty chest shook.

Gregor made no move to enter the room, instead he leaned from the inside against the wing of the door that was bolted fast, so that only half his body and the head inclined sideways above it could be seen as he peered across at the others. Meanwhile it had grown much lighter out; on the far side of the street, a section of the infinitely long, dark gray building opposite— a hospital—came into view with its regular windows punched into the facade; rain was still falling, but only in large drops that were separately visible and seemed to have been hurled one by one to the ground. An inordinate number of breakfast dishes crowded the table, for Gregor's father considered breakfast the most important meal of the day and would drag it out for hours reading various newspapers. Straight ahead, on the opposite wall, hung a photograph of Gregor from

his time in the military, showing him as a second lieu-
tenant whose carefree smile as he rested his hand on
his dagger commanded respect for his bearing and his
uniform. The door to the vestibule was open, and since
the front door was open as well, one could see all the
way out to the landing and the head of the stairs leading down.

"Well," Gregor said, quite conscious of the fact that
he was the only one who had retained his composure,
"I shall get dressed at once, pack up my samples and
be on my way. As for the rest of you, are you prepared
to let me do so? You can see, sir"—he said, addressing the general manager—"I am not obstinate, nor
a shirker; traveling is burdensome, but without it I
could not live. Where are you going now, sir? To the
office? Yes? Will you report all these things truthfully?
A person can be incapable of working at the moment,
but this is precisely the right time to recall his earlier
accomplishments and consider that he will later, once
the hindrance has been overcome, work all the more
industriously and with greater focus. I am so dreadfully
indebted to the boss, surely you're aware of this. On
the other hand, I have my parents and sister to think
of. Truly I'm in a bind, but I shall work my way out of

it. Don't make things more difficult for me than they already are. Take my side at the office! No one loves us drummers, I know. Everyone thinks the salesmen rake in a king's ransom while enjoying life's pleasures. And there's never any particular cause to reconsider this prejudice. But you, sir, have a far better grasp of the general circumstances than the rest of the staff, better even—if I may speak confidentially—than the boss himself, who in his role as businessman can easily err in his opinion to an employee's disadvantage. And you no doubt know quite well that a drummer, who spends almost the entire year away from the office, can easily become the victim of gossip, happenstance and groundless complaints against which he cannot possibly defend himself, as he usually never even learns of them, or only when he has completed one of his journeys, exhausted, and then back at home is forced to observe the dire physical effects of causes that can no longer be identified. Please, sir, do not leave without saying something to show you agree with me at least to some small extent!"

But the general manager had already turned away as soon as Gregor began to speak, and merely glanced back at him over a hunched shoulder, his mouth contorted. And during Gregor's speech he did not stand still for a moment but instead continued to retreat— not letting Gregor out of his sight—in the direction of the door, but only gradually, as though it were secretly prohibited to exit this room. Already he was in the vestibule, and to judge by the abrupt motion with which he withdrew his foot from the living room for the last time, one might have supposed he'd just burned it. Having reached the vestibule, however, he stretched out his right hand, gesturing broadly in the direction of the stairs, as if some all but supernatural salvation awaited him there.

Gregor realized he could not possibly allow the general manager to depart in his present frame of mind if his own position at the firm was not to be put in the gravest jeopardy. His parents didn't fully comprehend his situation: over these long years they had formed the conviction that Gregor was provided for in this office for life, and besides they were so preoccupied with their present worries that they were bereft of all foresight. But Gregor had this foresight. The general manager would have to be detained, reasoned with, convinced and finally won over; after all, Gregor's future and that of his family depended on it. If only his sister were here! She was clever; she had already begun to weep while Gregor was still lying quietly on his back. And surely the general manager, ever the ladies' man, would have let himself be assuaged by her; she would have closed the front door of the apartment and talked him out of his fear in the vestibule. But his sister was not there, so Gregor himself would have to act. And without stopping to consider that he was not yet familiar with his current abilities with respect to locomotion, nor even taking into account the fact that this last speech of his had quite possibly—indeed probably—eluded comprehension, he let go of the door; forced his way through the opening; meant to walk over to where the general manager, already out on the landing, was foolishly clutching at the banister with both hands; but right away, groping in vain for something to catch hold of, he fell with a faint shriek upon his many little legs. No sooner had this occurred than he felt—for the first time all morning—a sense of physical well-being; his legs had solid ground beneath them; they obeyed his will perfectly, as he noted to his delight; they even strove to bear him wherever he wished; and already it seemed to him he would soon be delivered from all his sufferings. But as he lay there on the floor directly in front of his mother and not far from her, swaying with mobility held in check, she suddenly leapt up—rapt as she had appeared within her own contemplations— leapt high up into the air, her arms thrust wide, fingers spread, crying out: "Help me, for God's sake, help!" her head cocked at an angle, as if to see Gregor better, but then, contradicting this, she senselessly retreated; but she had forgotten the table set for breakfast just behind her; sat down hurriedly upon it as soon as she reached it, as if absentmindedly; and didn't seem to notice that the big overturned coffeepot beside her was pouring a thick stream of coffee on the rug.

"Mother, Mother," Gregor said softly, gazing up at her. For a moment he had forgotten all about the general manager; on the other hand, he could not restrain himself, when he beheld this flowing coffee, from snapping his jaws several times. At this, the mother gave another shriek and fled from the table into the arms of Gregor's father as he rushed to her aid. But Gregor had no time for his parents now; the general manager was already on the stairs; his chin propped on the banister, he looked back on the scene one last time. Gregor was just preparing to dash after him to be sure of catching up with him; but the manager must have sensed something, for he leapt down several steps at once and vanished; and the cry of horror he gave as he fled resounded through the stairwell. Unfortunately the manager's flight now appeared to utterly discombobulate Gregor's father, who up till then had been relatively composed, for instead of running after the manager himself or at least not hindering Gregor in his own pursuit, he seized the manager's walking stick in one hand—it had been left lying on an armchair along with his overcoat and hat—with the other took up a large newspaper from the table, and set about driving Gregor back into his room with a great stamping of feet, brandishing both newspaper and stick. All Gregor's entreaties were in vain, nor were they even understood, for as submissively as he might swivel his head, his father only stamped his feet all the more ferociously. Across the room, his mother had flung open a window despite the chilly weather, and, leaning out, she pressed her face into her hands far outside the window frame. Between street and stairwell, a powerful draft arose, the window curtains flew into the air, the newspapers on the table rustled, and a few pages scudded across the floor. Inexorably Gregor's father drove him backward, uttering hissing sounds like a wild

man. But Gregor had no practice at all in reverse locomotion, and his progress was very slow. If only he'd
been permitted to turn around, he'd have been back
in his room at once, but he was afraid of provoking his
father's fury with this time-consuming maneuver, and
at any moment a fatal blow from the stick in his father's
hand might come crashing down on his back or head.
In the end, though, he had no alternative: horrified, he
realized he was incapable of controlling his direction;
and so he began, with constant anxious glances back at
his father, to turn around as quickly as he could, which
in fact was rather slowly. Perhaps his father discerned
his good intentions, for he did not hinder him in this
operation but instead even guided his rotation here and
there from a distance, using the tip of his stick. If only
his father were not making that unbearable hissing
noise! It made Gregor lose his head completely. He had
already turned almost all the way around when—still
with this hissing in his ear—he became confused and
started turning back in the wrong direction. But when
finally he succeeded in positioning his head in front of
the doorway, it turned out that his body was too wide
to fit through the opening. And of course in his father's
current state it could not possibly have occurred to him

to open the door's other wing to create an adequate passage. He was fixated on the notion that Gregor must disappear into his room as quickly as possible. Never would he have tolerated the complicated preparations necessary for Gregor to prop himself up so as possibly to pass through the door in an upright position. Instead, as though there were no obstacle at all, he now drove Gregor before him, raising a great din: what Gregor heard at his back no longer resembled the voice of merely a single father; it was do or die, and Gregor thrust himself—come what would—into the doorway. One side of his body tilted up, rising at an angle as he pressed forward, scraping his one flank raw and leaving ugly stains behind on the white door, and soon he was wedged tight, unable to move on his own; on one side, his little legs dangled trembling in midair, while on the other they were crushed painfully beneath him—then his father administered a powerful shove from behind, a genuinely liberating thrust that sent him flying, bleeding profusely, into the far reaches of his room. The door was banged shut with the stick, and then at last all was still.

II

ONLY AS DUSK WAS FALLING DID GREGOR WAKE from his heavy, faintlike sleep. He probably wouldn't have slept much longer even without a disturbance, for he felt sufficiently rested and restored, but it seemed to him he had been woken by a fleeting step and the careful shutting of the door to the vestibule. The pallid gleam of the electric streetlamps touched the ceiling here and there and the upper edges of the furniture, but down where Gregor lay, all was dark. Slowly, groping awkwardly with his feelers, which he was only now learning to appreciate, he dragged himself toward the door, wanting to see what had happened. His left side felt like one long unpleasantly contracting scar, and he was forced to limp outright on his two rows of legs. One of these diminutive legs, incidentally, had suffered grievous injuries in the course of the morning's events—it was almost miraculous only one had been injured—and now trailed lifelessly behind him.

Not until he reached the door did he realize what in fact had lured him there: it was the smell of something edible. There stood a bowl filled with sweet milk in which little pieces of white bread were floating. He almost laughed with delight, for his hunger was now even more powerful than in the morning, and right away he dunked his head in the milk almost up to his eyes. But he quickly drew it out again in disappointment; it wasn't just that eating was difficult thanks to his tender left side—and he couldn't eat at all without his entire body becoming gaspingly involved—but beyond that: even though milk had always been his favorite drink, which is no doubt why his sister had brought him some, now it didn't taste good to him at all, indeed it was almost with revulsion that he turned away from the bowl and crept back to the center of the room.

In the living room, as Gregor saw through the crack, the gas had been lit, but while usually at this hour his father liked to read aloud from the afternoon paper to Gregor's mother and sometimes his sister as well in a dramatic voice, now there was not a sound to be heard. Well, perhaps this customary reading aloud that his sister had often told and written him about had recently fallen out of practice. But even in the other rooms everything was so still, even though the apartment was surely not empty. "What a quiet life my family has been leading," Gregor said to himself, and as he gazed fixedly into the darkness before him, he felt great pride at having been able to give his parents and sister a life like this in such a beautiful apartment. But what if all this tranquility, all this prosperity and contentment were now coming to a horrific end? So as not to get lost in such contemplations, Gregor set himself in motion, crawling back and forth across the room.

Once in the course of this long evening one of the side doors was opened a tiny crack and then quickly shut again, and once the other one; someone must have felt an urge to enter and then been overcome by misgivings. Gregor now stationed himself just in front of the living room door, determined to somehow coax the hesitant visitor inside or at least find out who it was; but the door did not open again, and Gregor waited in vain. Before, when all the doors were locked, everyone kept trying to come in, and now that he had opened the one door and the others had apparently been opened during the day, no one came, and the keys were sticking in their locks from the outside.

It was late at night by the time the light in the living room went out, and now it was easy to ascertain that Gregor's parents and sister had remained awake all this time, for all three of them could clearly be heard departing on tiptoe. Now it was unlikely anyone would come into Gregor's room before morning; so he had plenty of time to ponder how best to reorder his life. But this high open room in which he was forced to lie flat on the floor distressed him, without his being able to determine the cause—after all, it was his room, which he had been living in for five years now—and with a half-unconscious motion, and not without a twinge of shame, he scurried beneath the settee, where even though his back was a bit cramped and he could no longer raise his head, he at once felt right at home, his only regret being that his body was too wide across to be accommodated entirely beneath this piece of furniture.

Here he remained the entire night, which he spent by turns dozing—though he was woken again and again by his hunger—and mulling over his worries and indistinct hopes, which however all led to the conclusion that, for the time being, he should behave calmly and, by employing patience and the utmost consideration, assist his family in enduring the inconveniences his current state inevitably forced him to impose on them.

Early the next morning already, so early it was almost still night, Gregor had the opportunity to test the strength of these resolutions he had made, for from the vestibule his sister, almost completely clothed, opened his door and cast an anxious glance into the room. She didn't immediately spot him, but when she noticed him beneath the settee—well, goodness, he had to be somewhere, it's not as if he might have flown away—the sight so alarmed her that, unable to control herself, she slammed the door from the outside. But as if regretting this conduct, she opened it again at once and came in, walking on tiptoe as though she were entering the room of a gravely ill patient or even a stranger. Gregor, having slid his head to just beneath the edge of the settee, observed her. Would she see that he had left the milk standing, and not because of a lack of hunger, and would she bring him some other food more to his liking? If she failed to do so of her own accord, he would sooner starve than call this to her attention, though in fact he felt a nearly monstrous urge to scoot out from beneath the settee, throw himself at his sister's feet, and beg her for something good to eat. But his sister immediately remarked with surprise that the bowl was still full, with just a little of its milk spilled on the floor around it, and she picked it up right away—not with her bare hands, to be sure, but with a rag—and carried it out of the room. Gregor was exceptionally curious to see what she would bring in its stead and mulled over various possibilities. But never would he have been able to predict what his sister in her kindness proceeded to do. To gauge his tastes, she brought him an entire assortment of foodstuffs, all spread out on an old newspaper. There were old, half-rotten vegetables; bones from the family supper the night before caked in a congealed white sauce; a few raisins and almonds; a piece of cheese Gregor had declared inedible two days before; a dry piece of bread; a slice of buttered bread; and a slice of bread with butter and salt. In addition, she placed beside this feast the bowl that apparently had been reserved for Gregor once and for all; it was now filled with water. And out of delicacy, since she knew Gregor would not eat in front of her, she quickly withdrew and even turned the key in the lock so that Gregor would understand he could make himself at home. Gregor's little legs whirred as he now went to take his meal. His wounds, incidentally, seemed to have healed entirely in the meantime, for he no longer felt the least impairment; this was astonishing, for more than a month ago he had cut his finger just a tiny bit with a knife, and this wound had still been painful enough just the day before yesterday. "Might I be less fastidious than before?" he thought, already sucking greedily at the cheese, to which he'd found himself immediately, inexorably drawn, more than to any of the other items. Quickly, his eyes shedding tears of gratification, he devoured in swift succession: the cheese, the vegetables, and the sauce; the fresh food, by contrast, did not taste good to him, in fact he could not even stand the smell of it and so dragged the things he wished to eat a little to one side. He had long since finished everything and was just lying indolently where he was when his sister slowly turned the key in the lock as a signal for him to withdraw. At once he gave a start, though he'd been on the point of nodding off, and he hurried back under the settee. But it cost him a great deal of willpower to remain there even for the short period of time his sister spent in the room, for the hearty meal he'd enjoyed had caused his abdomen to swell, and he could scarcely breathe in his confinement. In between little attacks of suffocation, he peered out with slightly bulging eyes as his sister, oblivious, used a broom to sweep up not only the remains of his meal but also the food he hadn't even touched, as if these items too were no longer fit for consumption, then she hastily dumped everything in a bucket that she covered with a wooden lid before carrying it all out of the room again. She had scarcely turned her back when Gregor hauled himself out from under the settee, stretching and puffing up his body.

This was how Gregor now received his food each day, once in the morning, when his parents and the maid were still asleep, and the second time after everyone had eaten lunch, for his parents would always nap a little afterward, and his sister would send the maid out on some errand or other. Surely they didn't want Gregor to starve either, but perhaps it would have been too much for them to experience his meals through more than hearsay, or perhaps his sister wanted to spare them even this modest sorrow, for Lord knows they were suffering enough.

Gregor never learned on what pretext the doctor and locksmith had been sent away that first morning, for since he himself could not be understood, it occurred to no one, not even his sister, that he could understand the others, so when his sister came to his room, he had to be content merely with hearing the sighs she heaved now and then and her words of supplication addressed to the saints. Only later, when she had started to grow accustomed to all of this—though of course it was impossible to become fully accustomed to circumstances like these—would Gregor sometimes catch a remark that was meant in a friendly way or could be interpreted as such. "He tucked right in today," she would say when Gregor had found the food she left him particularly tasty, while in the opposite case, which gradually began to occur more and more often, she was in the habit of saying almost mournfully: "This time he didn't touch a thing."

But while no news reached Gregor directly, he sometimes was able to overhear this and that from the rooms to either side of his, and whenever he heard voices, he would immediately run over to the door in question and press his entire body against it. Especially in the early days there was rarely a conversation that did not somehow, if only indirectly, refer to him. For two days, every mealtime was spent deliberating how the family should now comport itself; but even between meals this same discussion continued, for at least two members of the household were present at all times, since apparently no one wanted to remain at home alone, and of course leaving the apartment unattended was out of the question. What's more, the maid had fallen on her knees before Gregor's mother that very first day—it was not entirely clear what and how much she knew of what had occurred—begging to be released from the family's service, and when she took her leave a quarter of an hour later, she tearfully thanked them for dismissing her, as though this were the greatest benefaction she had experienced at their hands, and without anyone asking this of her, she swore a solemn oath never to reveal anything at all to anyone.

Now Gregor's sister was forced to do the cooking in concert with his mother; to be sure, not much effort was involved, as no one did much eating. Again and again Gregor would hear one of them pressing the others to eat—always in vain, and never with any other response than "Thank you, I've had all I want," or similar words. Perhaps they didn't drink anything either. Often Gregor's sister would ask her father if he wouldn't like a beer, affectionately offering to fetch it herself, and when he did not respond, she would say, wishing to relieve him of all scruples, that she could send the porter's wife for it as well, but then the father would utter a great "No," and no one spoke of it any longer.

Already in the course of the first day, Gregor's father explained the family's finances and prospects not only to Gregor's mother but to his sister as well. Now and then he would get up from the table and, from his small Wertheim safe, which he had salvaged when his business collapsed five years before, extract some receipt or memorandum book. One could hear him opening the complicated lock and then bolting it shut again after removing the desired item. These explanations on his father's part included the first bits of heartening news Gregor had heard since his captivity began. He had been under the impression that his father had retained nothing at all of his former firm's holdings, or at least his father had never said anything to the contrary, and admittedly Gregor himself had never asked him about this. At the time, his only concern had been to do everything in his power to let the family forget, as quickly as possible, the mercantile catastrophe that had plunged all of them into a state of utter hopelessness. And so he had set to work with particular zeal and risen almost overnight from petty clerk to salesman, in which capacity of course he had a quite different earning potential, and his professional accomplishments, in the form of commissions, were immediately transformed into cash that could be plunked down on the table at home, before the eyes of his astonished, delighted family. Those had been lovely times, and never since had they been repeated, at least not with such glory, although Gregor later earned so much money that he was in a position to cover the expenses for the entire family, which he then did. All had grown accustomed to this arrangement, not just the family but Gregor as well: they gratefully accepted the money, and he was happy to provide it, but the exchange no longer felt particularly warm. Only Gregor's sister had remained close to him all this time, and it was his secret plan to send her off to study at the Conservatory next year (unlike Gregor, she dearly loved music and could play the violin quite movingly), despite the considerable costs this would no doubt entail, money that could surely be brought in by other means. Often during the brief periods of time Gregor spent in town, the Conservatory would come up in his conversations with his sister, but only ever as a lovely dream whose realization was unthinkable, and their parents did not like to hear it mentioned even in this innocuous way; but Gregor was thinking the matter over with great determination and intended to make a formal announcement on Christmas Eve.

Thoughts like these, utterly futile in his current state, passed through his head as he stood pressed against the door, eavesdropping. Sometimes general exhaustion made it impossible for him to go on listening, and he would carelessly let his head bump against the door, but then he would immediately hold his head still again, for even the faint sound this produced had been heard in the next room, causing everyone to fall silent. "I wonder what he's getting up to now," his father would say after a while, apparently facing the door, and only then would the interrupted conversation resume.

Gregor now learned, and learned quite well (his father tended to repeat himself in his explanations, in part because it had been so long since he'd last concerned himself with such matters, in part because Gregor's mother did not always understand everything the first time), that despite all their misfortunes, a small nest egg—really only a tiny one—still remained to them from before, and had even grown a little thanks to the untouched interest that had accumulated meanwhile. In addition, the money Gregor had brought home each month—he only ever kept a few gulden for himself—had not yet been entirely used up and had grown into a small capital. Behind his door, Gregor nodded eagerly, delighted at this unexpected prudence and thrift. To be sure, he might have used this surplus to pay off more of his father's debts with his boss, and the day on which he would have been able to divest himself of his post would no longer have been nearly so far off, but as things stood, his father's arrangements were no doubt for the best.

Now this money was by no means sufficient to allow the family to live off the interest or anything of that sort; it might possibly have been enough to sustain the family for a year, two at most, but that's all there was. So in fact it was the kind of sum one really shouldn't touch, one to be set aside in case of emergency; the money to live on would have to be earned. Gregor's father was admittedly in good health, but he was old and hadn't worked in a full five years, and in any case he was supposed to avoid overtaxing himself; in those five years—the first holiday in his strenuous and yet unsuccessful life—he had put on a lot of weight and now lumbered as he walked. And was Gregor's old mother now supposed to hold down a job, despite her asthma and the fact that it was already an exertion for her to cross from one end of the apartment to the other, for which reason she spent every second day gasping for breath on the sofa beside the open window? And was his sister to go out working, this child of seventeen whose lifestyle no one would begrudge her: dressing nicely, sleeping late, helping out around the house, taking part in a few modest entertainments, and above all, playing the violin? Whenever the family came to speak of the necessity of someone earning money, Gregor would let go of the door and throw himself down upon the cool leather sofa beside it, burning with shame and sorrow.

Often he would lie there the entire long night, not sleeping for a moment, just scrabbling for hours against the leather. Or, not shunning the great effort it cost him to push an armchair over to the window, he would climb up the sill and, propped in the armchair, lean against the window, apparently lost in some sort of reverie of how liberating he'd always found it to gaze outside. For in truth he saw even the objects that were quite near at hand less and less clearly as the days progressed; the hospital across the way whose all too constant sight he had earlier reviled was now no longer even visible to him, and if he had not known perfectly well that he was a resident of Charlottenstrasse, a quiet but perfectly urban street, he might have imagined he was gazing out his window onto a desert in which the gray sky and the gray earth were indistinguishably conjoined. His attentive sister only had to see the armchair standing beside the window twice before she started pushing it back to its place there each time she tidied his room; indeed she even began leaving the window's inner sash open.

If only Gregor had been able to speak to his sister and thank her for all she was compelled to do for him, he would have found her ministrations easier to bear; as it was, he suffered beneath them. His sister, to be sure, did all she could to obscure the awkwardness of the situation, and the more time passed, the better she succeeded, of course, but Gregor came to see it all more and more clearly. Even the way she made her entrance jangled his nerves. The moment she came in, without even pausing to shut the door—although she always took such pains to shield the others from

the sight of Gregor's room—she would race straight-
away to the window and fling it open with hasty hands
as though she were on the point of suffocating, then
remain standing there, however cold it might be, gulp-
ing in the air. All this racing and racket was inflicted
on Gregor twice a day; he would be trembling beneath
the settee, painfully aware that she would no doubt
have willingly spared him this disruption if it were
possible for her to endure being in the same room as
Gregor with the window closed.

Once—it must have been a month since Gregor's
metamorphosis, so there was no particular call for
his sister to be startled by his appearance—she came
into his room a little earlier than usual and discovered
him, motionless and propped upright as if for horrific
effect, gazing out the window. Gregor would not have
found it surprising if she had chosen not to enter, since
his position prevented her from opening the window
right away, but she didn't just not enter: she started in
alarm and shut the door; a stranger might have thought
Gregor had been lying in wait, meaning to bite her.
Gregor naturally went and hid himself away beneath
the settee, but he had to wait there until noon before his
sister returned, and she seemed far more agitated than

usual. From this he understood that his appearance was still unbearable to her and would remain so, and that she no doubt had to struggle to force herself not to run away at the sight of even the small part of his body that protruded from beneath the settee. In order to spare her even this sight, one day he carried the bedsheet over to the settee on his back—this labor cost him four hours—and arranged it in such a way that he was now completely covered, so that his sister would not be able to see him even if she bent down. If she considered the sheet unnecessary, she could have removed it, since it was clear enough that it could not possibly be considered a pleasure for Gregor to shut himself off so completely, but she left the sheet where it was, and Gregor even thought he glimpsed a grateful look when at one point he carefully lifted the sheet just a little with his head to see how his sister liked the new arrangement.

During the first fortnight, Gregor's parents could not bring themselves to enter his room, and often he heard them expressing their heartfelt appreciation of his sister's labors, whereas earlier they had often been annoyed with her, since she had seemed to them a rather useless girl. But now both of them, father and mother alike, would often be waiting just outside

Gregor's door while his sister tidied up his room, and as soon as she emerged, she had to give a full report on what things looked like in the room, what Gregor had eaten, how he had behaved this time, and whether perhaps any modest improvement could be seen. His mother, incidentally, had wanted to visit him relatively soon, but his father and sister held her back, appealing at first to her sense of reason as Gregor listened attentively, wholeheartedly approving. Later, though, she had to be held back by force, and when she then cried out: "Let me go to Gregor, he is my unhappy son! Can't you understand that I must go to him?" then Gregor thought it would perhaps be good for his mother to visit him, not every day of course, but perhaps once a week; after all, she had a far better grasp of things than his sister, who despite her courage was still a child and, when it came right down to it, had perhaps only taken on this difficult task out of childish frivolity.

Gregor's wish to see his mother was soon fulfilled. During the day, Gregor avoided showing himself at the window, if only out of consideration for his parents, but there wasn't much crawling he could do in the few square meters of space the floor provided, lying still was already difficult for him to endure during the night, eating had soon ceased to give him even the slightest pleasure, and so to divert himself he took up the habit of crawling back and forth across the walls and ceiling. He particularly liked hanging from the ceiling high above the room; it was completely different from lying on the floor; one could breathe more freely there; a gentle swaying motion rocked the body; and in the almost happy absentmindedness Gregor experienced, it might happen, to his own astonishment, that he would let go and crash to the floor. But now, of course, he had his body far better under control than before, and even as great a fall as this did him no harm. His sister immediately noticed the new entertainment Gregor had devised for himself—his peregrinations left behind sticky trails here and there—and she got it into her head to make it possible for Gregor to range as widely as possible by removing the furniture that impeded his movement, above all the wardrobe and desk. But she wasn't able to do so on her own; she didn't dare ask her father for help; the maid most certainly would not have helped her, for this girl of sixteen or so, though she had courageously remained in the household after the departure of the former cook, had at the same time requested the privilege of keeping the kitchen locked at all times and only opening the door upon particular request; and so the sister had no choice but to summon her mother one day when her father was out. The mother arrived with exclamations of feverish joy but fell silent at the door to Gregor's room. At first, of course, Gregor's sister checked to confirm that all in the room was as it should be; only then did she allow her mother to enter. With the utmost haste, Gregor had tugged the sheet down lower and in looser folds so that it really did look as if a bedsheet just happened to have been tossed over the settee. He also refrained from peering out from beneath the sheet this time; for the moment, he would resign himself to not seeing his mother and just be glad she had come. "It's all right, come in, you won't see him," Gregor's sister said, apparently leading her mother by the hand. Gregor now heard the sounds of these two weak women grappling with this in fact quite heavy old wardrobe, with his sister laying claim to the bulk of the work, not listening to the admonitions of her mother, who was afraid she would overtax herself. It took a very long time. After perhaps a quarter of an hour's labor, Gregor's mother said they should leave the wardrobe where it was after all; in the first place, it was too heavy—they would not finish before

Gregor's father came home, and by leaving the wardrobe in the middle of the room, they would prevent Gregor from moving around at all—and secondly, it wasn't even clear they were doing him a favor by taking away the furniture. To her, it seemed the opposite was true: the sight of the empty wall positively oppressed her heart; and why should Gregor not experience this same sentiment, since after all he was long accustomed to having this furniture around him—wouldn't he feel abandoned in an emptied-out room? "And is it not as if," his mother concluded in a low voice—in fact, she had been whispering all along, as though she wished to avoid letting Gregor, whose exact whereabouts she did not know, hear so much as the sound of her voice, for she was convinced he could not understand her words—"and is it not as if by removing the furniture we would be showing that we are giving up all hope of a cure and are ruthlessly abandoning him to his own devices? I think it would be best if we try to keep the room in precisely the same state it was in before, so that when Gregor returns to us he will find everything unchanged, which will make it that much easier for him to forget all that has happened in the meantime."

Hearing his mother's words, Gregor realized that the

absence of all direct human address, combined with the monotony of life in his family's midst, must have muddled his understanding over the course of these two months, for he could not otherwise explain to himself how he could seriously have wished to have his room emptied out. Did he really want to have this warm room, comfortably furnished with family heirlooms, transformed into a cave or den—in which, to be sure, he would be able to crawl about unhindered in every direction, but at the price of simultaneously swiftly and completely forgetting his human past? He was already on the verge of forgetting, and only his mother's voice, which he had gone so long now without hearing, had shaken him awake. Nothing should be removed; everything must remain; he was unwilling to forego the good influence this furniture had on his condition; and if the furniture got in the way of his practicing this mindless crawling about, this was by no means to his detriment, in fact, it was a great advantage.

Unfortunately his sister was of a different opinion; she had developed the habit—not entirely without cause, to be sure—of presenting herself as the holder of particular expertise when discussing Gregor with her parents, and so now too her mother's counsel was reason enough for her to insist on the removal not only of the wardrobe and desk, as she had originally been intending, but of every last bit of the room's furnishings, with the exception of the indispensable settee. Naturally, it was not simply childish defiance and the hard-won self-assurance she had so unexpectedly acquired in recent weeks that dictated this demand; she had, in fact, observed that Gregor needed a great deal of space to crawl around in, while as far as anyone could see, he made no use whatever of the furniture. But perhaps the fanciful imagination of a girl of her age played a role as well, a sensibility always seeking its own gratification, and one which Grete now allowed to persuade her to render Gregor's situation even more horrific than before, so as to be able to do even more for him than she had hitherto. For a room in which Gregor held sole dominion over empty walls was a place where no one other than Grete would ever dare to set foot.

And so she held fast to her resolve despite the protests of her mother, who appeared troubled to the point of indecision even by the room in its present state; she soon fell silent and helped Gregor's sister remove the wardrobe as best she could. Well, the wardrobe was something Gregor could do without if need be, but the desk would certainly have to stay. And no sooner had the women left the room with the cabinet, groaning as they pressed against its weight, than Gregor poked out his head from beneath the settee to see how he might, cautiously and as considerately as possible, intervene. But unfortunately his mother was the first to return while Grete was still in the next room, clasping the wardrobe in her arms and tipping it back and forth on her own—without, of course, moving it from the spot. But Gregor's mother was unaccustomed to his appearance, it might have made her ill to catch a glimpse of him, and so Gregor in alarm withdrew as fast as he could to the far end of the settee, but it was too late to prevent the front edge of the bedsheet from stirring a little. This was enough to attract his mother's notice. Startled, she froze for a moment, then went back to where Grete was.

Although Gregor kept telling himself that nothing extraordinary was happening, just a few sticks of furniture being shifted about, he was soon forced to admit that all this coming and going on the part of the women, their little exclamations, the furniture scraping against the floor, had the combined effect of a tumultuous hubbub intensifying all around him, and no matter how tightly he drew his head and legs in and pressed his body against the floor, he soon was forced to consider that he would not be able to endure this much longer. They were clearing out his room; taking from him all that was dear to him; they had already borne away the cabinet in which lay his fretsaw and other tools; and now they were prying loose the desk that had dug itself firmly into the floorboards, this desk at which he had written his homework assignments as a student at the commercial academy, and as a secondary and even primary school pupil—truly there was no time left to explore the good intentions of these two women, whose existence, by the way, he had almost forgotten, for their exhaustion was now making them labor in silence, and one heard only their heavy footsteps.

And so he burst out of hiding—the women in the next room were just leaning on the desk to catch their breath—changing direction four times as he raced about, for he really didn't know what to save first, but then his eyes lit on the picture of the lady clad all in furs, conspicuous now on the otherwise empty wall, and quickly he made his way up to it and pressed himself against the glass, which adhered to him, pleasantly cool against his hot belly. At least this picture, which Gregor's body now covered up completely, was abso-

lutely certain not to be taken away from him. He swiv-
eled his head toward the living room door to observe
the women as they returned.

They hadn't permitted themselves much rest at all
and were already on their way back; Grete had slung one
arm about her mother and was nearly carrying her. "So
what should we take next?" Grete said, looking around.
Then her eyes met those of Gregor where he clung to
the wall. It was no doubt only because of her mother's
presence that she kept her composure; bowing her face
toward her mother to prevent her from glancing about,
she said—hastily and trembling, to be sure—"Let's go
back to the living room for a moment, shall we?" Grete's
intentions were perfectly clear to Gregor: she meant to
bring their mother to safety and then chase him from the
wall. Well, let her try! He sat there on his picture and
would not give it up. He'd sooner leap right in her face.

But Grete's words succeeded in unsettling her
mother even more: taking one step to the side, she saw
the huge brown blotch on the flowered wallpaper, and
before she was even able to realize that what she saw
there was Gregor, she cried out in a hoarse, shrieking
voice, "Oh God, oh God!" and fell back upon the settee, her arms spread wide as though she were giving up

everything, and lay there without moving. "Gregor!" his sister shouted, raising her fist with a threatening glower. It was the first time she had addressed him directly since his metamorphosis. She ran into the next room to fetch some sort of essence that could be used to awaken her mother from her faint; Gregor wanted to help as well—there would be time enough to save the picture later—but he stuck fast to the glass and had to tear himself away by force; he too then ran into the next room as if he might offer his sister advice of some sort, like in the old days; but then could only stand idly behind her as she rummaged among various little bottles, and scared her out of her wits when she turned around; one bottle flew to the floor and shattered; a shard of glass scratched Gregor's face, and some sort of corrosive medicine engulfed him; without further delay, Grete took up as many bottles as she could hold and ran with them to her mother, slamming the door behind her with her foot. Gregor was now cut off from his mother, who was possibly on the brink of death, for which he himself was to blame; he could not open the door if he didn't want to drive away his sister, who had to stay there with his mother; there was nothing for him to do but wait; and tormented by his worries and self-reproach, he began to crawl about, crawling over everything, walls, furniture, the ceiling, and finally in his despair, as the entire room began to spin around him, he fell smack in the middle of the big table.

A short while passed. Gregor lay there, spent, and around him all was still, possibly a good sign. Then the bell rang. The maid was naturally locked up in her kitchen and so Grete had to open the door. Their father was back. "What happened?" were his first words; the look on Grete's face had no doubt revealed all. Grete's voice as she responded was muffled, apparently she was pressing her face against his chest: "Mother fainted, but she's better already. Gregor has broken out." "That's just what I expected," the father said. "I kept telling you, but you women refused to listen." To Gregor it was clear his father had misinterpreted Grete's all too brief pronouncement to assume him guilty of some act of violence. So it behooved Gregor to try to pacify his father, as he was lacking both the time and means to enlighten him. With this in mind, he fled to the door of his room and pressed himself against it, so that the moment his father came into the living room from the vestibule he would see that Gregor had every intention of returning at once to his room, that it was unnecessary to drive him back inside, and that one had merely to open the door, and he would disappear at once.

But his father was in no mood to take note of subtleties. "Ah!" he exclaimed upon entering, in a tone of voice suggesting he was at once furious and glad. Gregor pulled his head back from the door and turned it toward his father. He had truly not expected to see his father looking as he looked now standing before him; though to be sure the novelty of crawling about had distracted him recently from paying as much attention as before to the goings-on in the rest of the apartment, and really he ought to have been prepared to find a changed set of circumstances. Even so, even so: was this still his father? The same man who used to lie wearily entombed in his bed when Gregor set off on a business trip; who would greet him on the evening of his return sitting in an armchair in his nightshirt; who, incapable of rising, would merely raise his arms to signify his delight, and on the rare walks they still shared, a few Sundays each year and on major holidays, would trudge between Gregor and his mother, who themselves were already walking rather slowly, moving even a bit slower than they, bundled up in his old overcoat, always with his gingerly advancing cane and almost invariably coming to a halt and collecting his companions around him whenever he had something to say? Now he was standing properly erect; dressed in a smart blue uniform with gold buttons of the sort worn by porters in banking establishments; above the jacket's tall, stiff collar his powerful double chin unfurled; beneath bushy eyebrows, his black eyes peered out acutely and attentively; his once disheveled white hair had been painstakingly combed and parted until it gleamed. He tossed his cap, to which a gold monogram was affixed, probably that of a bank, across the entire room in a wide arc to land on the settee, then advanced grim-faced upon Gregor with the tips of his long uniform jacket flung back and his hands in his trouser pockets. He himself probably had no idea what he intended to do; at any rate, he raised up each foot unusually high, and Gregor marveled at the gigantic dimensions of his boot-soles. But he did not lose any time over them, having learned on the very first day of his new life that his father considered only the utmost severity appropriate for him. And so he fled from his father, hesitating whenever his father stopped short, and then rushing forward again as soon as he stirred. They circled the room several times in this manner without anything decisive occurring,

and indeed, given the slow speed at which this inter-
action was taking place, without its even having the
appearance of a chase. For this reason Gregor remained
at floor level for the time being, especially as he feared
his father might consider it particular wickedness on
his part if he were to take refuge on the walls or ceiling. To be sure, he was forced to realize he would not
be able to keep up even this pace for long, since each
time his father took a step, he himself had to execute
any number of motions. A shortness of breath began
to set in—even in his earlier life his lungs had been
none too reliable. As he now lurched along, reserving
all his strength for this continued flight, his eyes barely
open (and not thinking, in his stupefaction, that there
might be other ways of saving himself than running
across the floor, indeed he had almost forgotten he also
had the walls at his disposal, though here, to be sure,
they were obstructed by delicately carved furniture
full of jagged, pointy edges), all at once something flew
to the rug beside him, casually flung, and rolled across
his path. It was an apple; and already a second one
came flying after it; in horror, Gregor stopped in his
tracks; there was no point continuing to run now that
his father had decided to bombard him. He had filled

his pockets from the fruit bowl on the sideboard and now was tossing apple after apple in Gregor's direction, for the moment not even bothering to take particular aim. The petite red apples rolled around the floor as if electrified, knocking into each other. One lightly lobbed apple grazed Gregor's back and slid off again harmlessly. But it was immediately followed by another that embedded itself in his back. Gregor tried to drag himself forward, as if this sudden shocking pain might vanish with a change of place; but he felt nailed to the spot and collapsed there, his legs splaying out, all his senses in a state of utter bewilderment. He caught only a last glimpse of the door to his room flying open, his shrieking sister, and his mother running out of the room before her wearing only a chemise, for his sister had undressed the unconscious woman to let her breathe more freely, then he saw his mother rush to his father's side, her unfastened skirts slipping one by one from about her waist as she ran, saw her stumble across these skirts as she threw herself at his father and, embracing him, in perfect union with him—but now Gregor's vision began to fail him—she clasped her hands at the back of his father's head and pleaded with him to spare Gregor's life.

III

THE GRIEVOUS WOUND GREGOR HAD RECEIVED, which plagued him for over a month—the apple remained lodged there in his flesh, a visible memento, since no one dared to remove it—seemed to have reminded even his father that Gregor, despite his current lamentable, repulsive form, was a member of the family who should not be treated like an enemy, for family duty dictated that the others swallow down the disgust he aroused in them and show him tolerance, only tolerance.

And even though this wound cost Gregor some of
his mobility, probably for good, and for the time being
he required many, many minutes to hobble across his
room like an old invalid—crawling up the walls was
out of the question now—he was compensated for this
worsening of his condition by what seemed to him a
perfectly adequate substitute: as evening approached,
the door to the living room, on which he would start
keeping a sharp eye an hour or two beforehand, would
always be opened so as to permit him, lying in his
own dark room and invisible from the living room, to
watch the entire family sitting at the brightly lit table
and listen to their conversations now, as it were, in an
officially sanctioned capacity and thus quite differently
than before.

To be sure, these were no longer the animated conversations of earlier times that Gregor used to think
back on with a certain longing from various cramped
hotel rooms when it was time to throw himself,
exhausted, into the damp bedding. Now everything
was fairly quiet. Gregor's father would fall asleep in
his armchair soon after supper; his mother and sister
would admonish one another to silence; his mother,
bent far over beneath the light, would be sewing ladies'

underthings for a dress shop; his sister, who had taken a job as a salesgirl, was studying stenography and French in the evenings so as possibly to move to a better position later on. Sometimes Gregor's father would wake up and, as if unaware he had been sleeping, would say to Gregor's mother: "How long you've been sewing again today!" and then go right back to sleep, which would prompt Gregor's mother and sister to exchange weary smiles.

In a peculiar form of stubbornness, Gregor's father refused to take off his porter's uniform even at home; and while his nightshirt hung uselessly on its hook, he would slumber where he sat, fully clothed, as though he remained ready for service at all times and even here was awaiting his supervisor's call. As a result, his uniform, which had not been new to start with, soon forfeited much of its cleanliness, despite the care lavished on it by mother and sister, and Gregor would sometimes gaze for an entire evening at this stain-covered jacket resplendent with gold buttons, always highly polished, in which the old man slept in considerable discomfort but nonetheless soundly.

The moment the clock struck ten, Gregor's mother would attempt to rouse his father with a few hushed words and then persuade him to go to bed, for he would get no proper sleep sitting here, and sleep was something Gregor's father—who had to report for duty at six in the morning—desperately needed. But in keeping with the stubbornness that had taken hold of him when he started working as a porter, he always insisted on continuing to sit there at the table, even though he kept falling asleep, and then it was only with the greatest effort that he could be persuaded to exchange armchair for bed. Gregor's mother and sister could persist in their little admonishments as doggedly as they liked; for a quarter of an hour, he would just shake his head slowly, his eyes closed, without getting up. Gregor's mother would pluck at his sleeve, whispering cajoling words in his ear, and his sister would set aside her studies to come to her mother's aid, but to no avail. Gregor's father only settled deeper into his armchair. Only when the women gripped him beneath the arms would he open his eyes, looking by turns at mother and sister and saying: "What sort of life is this? Is this the peace and quiet of my old age?" Then, supported by the two women, he would rise, laboriously, as though he himself were receiving the brunt of this burden, and allow the women to escort him to the doorway, where he would shoo them away and continue on his own, while Gregor's mother hastily threw down her sewing and his sister her pen so they could run after him to offer further assistance. The household was ever further reduced; the maid was now let go after all; a bony giant of a charwoman with white hair flapping about her head came by in the morning and evening to perform the heaviest labors; everything else was handled by Gregor's mother along with all her sewing. It even came to pass that several pieces of jewelry that had been in the family—jewels Gregor's mother and sister had delighted in wearing at entertainments and festivities—were sold, as Gregor would learn in the evening when the price each piece had brought would be discussed. But their greatest lament was always that they were unable to leave this apartment, which was far too large for their current circumstances, since no one could imagine how Gregor might be moved. But Gregor understood that it was not only out of consideration for him that a move was being ruled out, since he could easily enough have been transported in a crate of appropriate size with a few air holes; the main thing keeping the family from moving to a new apartment was their complete sense of hopelessness and the thought that they had been struck with a misfortune such as no one else in their entire circle of relations and friends had ever experienced. They were fulfilling to the utmost the demands the world makes on the poor: Gregor's father fetched breakfast for the petty employees at the bank, his mother sacrificed herself for the underclothes of strangers, his sister ran back and forth behind the shop counter at her customers' behest, but this was all the strength they had. And the wound in Gregor's back would begin to ache anew when mother and sister, having brought his father to bed, would now return and, leaving their work where it lay, huddle close beside one another pressing their cheeks together; when Gregor's mother, gesturing toward his room, would say: "Shut the door now, Grete"; and when Gregor was left in the dark again while next door the two women intermingled their tears or else sat there tearless, staring down at the table.

Gregor spent his nights and days almost entirely without sleeping. Sometimes he thought about taking the family's affairs in hand again, just as he used to, the next time his door was opened; once more his boss and the general manager would appear before his mind's eye after all this time, the clerks and apprentices, the dull-witted hired man, two or three friends from other firms, a chambermaid from a provincial hotel (a sweet, fleeting specter), the shopgirl from a haberdashery whom he had courted earnestly but too slowly—all of these now appeared to him, interspersed with strangers or people already forgotten, but instead of coming to his aid and that of his family, every last one of them was unapproachable, and he was glad when they disappeared. At other times he would be not at all in a frame of mind to look after his family; instead he was filled with rage at how poorly he was attended to, and although he could not imagine anything he would have liked to eat, he plotted how he might gain access to the pantry so as to help himself to what—despite his total absence of hunger—was his due. Without bothering to consider how she might give Gregor particular pleasure, his sister would quickly thrust some randomly chosen foodstuff into his room with her foot on her way to work in the morning or at midday, only to sweep it out again at night with a quick swipe of the broom, paying no heed if the food had been only barely nibbled at or—as was most often the case now—not touched at all. Setting Gregor's room to rights, a task she now saved for the evenings, could not possibly have been done any more perfunctorily. Great streaks of dirt extended across the walls, with balls of dust and rubbish lying scattered about. At first when Gregor's sister came into his room he would position himself in corners particularly indicative of this problem—to reproach her, as it were, by his presence there. But he could just as well have spent entire weeks sitting there without any improvement on his sister's part; after all, she saw the dirt as plainly as he did, but had made up her mind to leave it be. At the same time, with a sensitivity that was new in her, one that had now taken hold of the family as a whole, she was on her guard to make sure the task of tidying Gregor's room was reserved for her. Once Gregor's mother had subjected his room to a thorough scrubbing, which she accomplished only after using up several buckets of water— admittedly, all this moisture was itself an affront to Gregor, who lay stretched out, bitter and immobile, upon the settee—but his mother did not escape punishment. For no sooner had his sister remarked the change in Gregor's room that evening than she ran into the living room, grievously insulted, and ignoring her mother's imploringly raised hands, set to weeping so violently that her parents—naturally her father was startled out of his chair—at first stood by helpless and astonished; until they too began to stir; on the right, Gregor's father reproached his mother for not having left the cleaning of Gregor's room to his sister; while on the left he shouted at Gregor's sister, threatening that she would never again be permitted to clean Gregor's room; while his mother attempted to drag his father, now so agitated he hardly recognized himself, into the bedroom; Gregor's sister, shaking with sobs, pummeled the table with her tiny fists; and Gregor hissed loudly in fury because it had occurred to no one to shut the door of his room to spare him this sight and commotion.

But even if Gregor's sister, who was exhausted by her professional work, had wearied of caring for Gregor as she'd previously done, there was absolutely no need for his mother to fill her shoes, and Gregor needn't have suffered neglect. For now the charwoman was here. This old widow—who had seen and survived the worst in her long life with the help of her sturdy bones—felt no particular repugnance toward Gregor. Without being at all inquisitive, she had once chanced to open the door to his room and, seeing Gregor, who had begun to run back and forth although no one was chasing him, she stood there staring in astonishment, her hands clasped across her lap. Ever since, she never failed to open the door a crack for a moment every morning and evening to look in on him. At the beginning she would call him over to her, saying things that were probably intended to sound friendly, like "Hey, over here, you old dung beetle!" or "Just look at the old dung beetle!" Thus addressed, Gregor gave no reply but instead remained where he was, immobile, as if the door had never been opened. If only this charwoman, instead of being allowed to disturb him uselessly at whim, had been given instructions to clean his room daily! Once, early in the morning—a heavy rain, perhaps already a portent of the coming spring, was beating against the windowpanes—Gregor became so infuriated when the charwoman started up again with her quips that he turned on her as if to attack, if admittedly slowly and decrepitly. But instead of being frightened, the charwoman just picked up a chair that was standing beside the door and held it high in the air; and as she stood there, her mouth gaping wide, her intention was clear: not to close her mouth again until the chair in her hand had come crashing down upon Gregor's back. "Aha, so that's as far as it goes?" she asked as Gregor turned around again, and she placed the chair calmly back in its corner.

Gregor now ate almost nothing at all. Only if he happened by chance to wander past the food that had been prepared for him might he playfully take a bite of something into his mouth, where he would hold it for hours and then usually spit it out again later. At first he thought it was his sorrow at the state of his room that prevented him from eating, but in fact he had resigned himself very quickly to the changes there. Everyone had gotten into the habit of using his room to store things there was no space for in other parts of the apartment, and now there were many such things, since one room of the apartment had been rented out to three lodgers. These solemn gentlemen—all three of them were bearded, as Gregor once noted, peering through the crack of the door—were scrupulously intent on having everything tidy, not just in their room but also, since they were now paying rent here, in the entire household, particularly the kitchen. They could not bear the presence of unnecessary, much less dirty items. Moreover, they had brought most of their own furnishings with them. For this reason, many things had become superfluous, things that could not be sold but were still too valuable to throw out. All of this found its way into Gregor's room. As did the ash box and the garbage pail from the kitchen. The charwoman, always in a great hurry, would simply fling any unserviceable item into Gregor's room; mercifully, Gregor generally saw only the object in question and the hand that held it. The charwoman may have intended at some point, when she had occasion or a free minute, to come collect these things, or else throw all of them out at once, but as it was they remained wherever they first landed, except when Gregor made his way through the refuse, stirring it around—at first out of necessity, since there was no room left for him to crawl about, but later with ever-increasing pleasure, though after these wanderings, which left him mortally exhausted and sad, he would spend hours without moving.

Since the lodgers sometimes also took their supper at home in the shared living room, the living room door remained shut on some evenings, but Gregor was happy to forgo having the door open; in fact, even when it was open, he sometimes failed to take advantage of it and instead, unbeknownst to his family, would remain lying in the darkest corner of his room. Once, however, the charwoman had left the door to the living room slightly ajar, and ajar it remained even when the lodgers came in that evening and struck a light. They sat down at the head of the table where in earlier times Gregor had sat with his father and mother, unfolded the napkins and took up their knives and forks. At once Gregor's mother appeared in the doorway with a serving dish filled with meat, and right behind her came his sister bearing a plate piled high with potatoes. A heavy vapor rose from the steaming food. The lodgers bent over the dishes that had been placed before them, as though wishing to inspect them before beginning their meal, and in fact the one who sat in the middle and appeared to be an authority figure to the other two cut off a piece of meat right there on the platter to check whether it was tender enough and didn't have to be sent back to the kitchen. He was satisfied, and Gregor's mother and sister, who had been watching nervously, now smiled with relief.

The family members themselves ate in the kitchen. Nonetheless Gregor's father visited the living room on his way to the kitchen and with a single bow, cap in hand, took a tour around the table. The lodgers all rose from their seats and mumbled into their beards. Left alone again, they ate in almost perfect silence. It struck

Gregor as peculiar that amid all the various sounds of this meal, one could also make out their champing teeth, as if to demonstrate to Gregor that a person needs teeth to eat and that even the most splendid jaws, if toothless, can accomplish nothing at all. "I'm hungry," Gregor said sorrowfully to himself, "but not for these things. Just look how these lodgers take their nourishment while I am wasting away!"

On this very evening—Gregor couldn't remember having heard the violin once in all this time—the sound of it was heard coming from the kitchen. The lodgers had already finished their evening meal, the one in the middle had pulled out a newspaper, giving each of the others a page, and now the three of them were reading, leaning back in their chairs and smoking. When the violin began to play, their interest was piqued, they got up from their chairs and tiptoed over to the doorway leading to the vestibule, where they stood in a tight cluster. The sounds of this activity must have traveled to the kitchen, for Gregor's father now called out: "Are the gentlemen disturbed by this playing? It can be silenced at once." "On the contrary," said the one in the middle, "would the young lady care to join us and play here in the living room, where it is much more comfortable and pleasant?" "Why, of course," Gregor's father exclaimed, as though he were the violinist. The gentlemen went back into the room and waited. Soon Gregor's father arrived with the music stand, his mother with the sheet music and his sister with the violin. His sister calmly prepared to play; his parents, who never rented out rooms in earlier days and therefore were treating these lodgers with exaggerated deference, did not even dare to sit in their own armchairs; his father leaned against the door, his right hand tucked between two buttons of his closed livery jacket; his mother, meanwhile, was offered an armchair by one of the lodgers, and since she left the chair where he had happened to place it, she sat off to one side in a corner.

Gregor's sister began to play; on either side, his father and mother attentively followed each movement of her hands. Attracted by her playing, Gregor had ventured a bit further than usual and was already sticking his head into the living room. It scarcely surprised him that he had become so inconsiderate of the others; earlier on, his considerateness had been a source of pride. And he had all the more reason to keep himself hidden away now: thanks to the dust that lay everywhere in his room and would swirl up at the slightest motion, he too was covered in dust; he dragged around threads, hair and food scraps clinging to his back and sides; his general indifference was far too great now for him to keep up with a habit he'd once practiced several times a day: flipping over so as to scrub his back against the rug. And despite his condition, he did not hesitate now to continue his advance a little way out onto the immaculate floor of the living room.

To be sure, no one paid him the slightest heed. The family was completely absorbed in the violin playing; the lodgers, on the other hand, having at first positioned themselves, hands in their trouser pockets, much too close behind his sister's music stand, so that they could all look at the sheet music, which surely must have distracted her, soon withdrew to the window, conversing in an undertone, and remained there, anxiously observed by Gregor's father. It appeared more than clear they had been disappointed in their expectation of hearing beautiful or entertaining violin music and now, tired of the whole performance, were continuing to tolerate this disturbance of their peace only out of politeness. Particularly the way in which all of them were blowing the smoke of their cigars high into the air from their noses and mouths suggested extreme agitation. And yet his sister's playing was so lovely. Her face was tilted to one side; searchingly, sadly, her eyes followed the lines of notes. Gregor crept a bit farther forward and ducked his head down close to the floor so as perhaps to catch her eye. Was he a beast, that music so moved him? He felt as if he were being shown the way to that unknown nourishment he craved. He was determined to creep all the way up to his sister, to pluck at her skirt and in this way indicate to her that she should come to his room with her violin, for no one here was rewarding her playing as he meant to reward her. He would not allow her to leave his room ever again, at least as long as he was alive; his horrific figure would, for the first time ever, be useful to him; he would be at all the doors of his room at once, growling at his attackers; but his sister should remain with him not by force but of her own free will; she should sit beside him on the settee, bend down, the better to hear, and he would confess to her that he'd had the firm intention of sending her to the Conservatory and that if the disaster had not disrupted his plans, he would have made a general announcement last Christmas—Christmas had passed now, hadn't it?—without letting himself be swayed by objections of any sort. After this declaration, his sister would be moved to the point of tears, and Gregor would raise himself to the height of her armpit and kiss her throat, which, now that she went to the office every day, she wore free of ribbon or collar.

"Herr Samsa!" the gentleman in the middle shouted at Gregor's father, and without wasting a single word, pointed his finger at Gregor, who was slowly advancing. The violin fell silent, the middle lodger at first just smiled and shook his head, turning toward his friends, then looked again at Gregor. Gregor's father apparently found the task of driving Gregor back into his room less urgent than that of calming the lodgers, despite the fact that they did not appear particularly worked up and seemed to be finding Gregor more entertaining than the music. He hurried over to them and tried with outspread arms to herd them back into their room, at the same time using his body to shield Gregor from their view. And now they did in fact become a little angry, though it was no longer clear whether this was on account of Gregor's father's behavior or the realization dawning on them that without their knowledge they had been sharing their home with a roommate of this sort. They demanded explanations of Gregor's father; now it was their turn to throw their arms into the air; they plucked uneasily at their beards and only slowly withdrew in the direction of their room. Meanwhile Gregor's sister, who had been standing there at a loss since her playing had been so unexpectedly interrupted—she still held violin and bow in her carelessly dangling hands, looking over at the notes as though she were continuing to play—all at once pulled herself together, laid her instrument in the lap of her mother, who still sat there in her armchair, her lungs heaving as she fought for breath, and ran into the next room, toward which the lodgers were now moving somewhat more quickly as Gregor's father urged them on. One saw how, beneath his sister's practiced hands, the beds' blankets and pillows flew into the air and into orderliness. Even before the lodgers reached the room, she had finished making up the beds and slipped out. Gregor's father appeared to be once more so firmly in the grip of his own stubbornness that he forgot the basic respect that, after all, he owed his tenants. He kept up his pressing and urging until, already standing in the doorway, the middle lodger thunderously stamped his foot, causing Gregor's father to stop short. "I hereby declare," he said, raising his hand and seeking out Gregor's mother and sister too as he glanced about, "that in consideration of the reprehensible circumstances prevailing in this apartment and family"—and here he spat on the floor without forethought—"I give notice on my room effective immediately. It goes without saying that I will not pay a penny for the days I have spent here; on the contrary, I shall consider whether or not to pursue you with— please believe me—easily justifiable claims." He fell silent and went on looking straight before him expectantly. And indeed his two friends at once chimed in with the words, "We too give notice effective immediately." Hereupon he seized the door handle and with a great crash slammed the door.

Gregor's father staggered to his armchair with groping hands and let himself fall into it; it looked as though he was stretching out for his customary evening nap, but the violent nodding of his anchorless head showed that he was absolutely not sleeping. Gregor had gone on lying quietly on the spot where the lodgers had espied him. His disappointment at the failure of his plan and perhaps also the weakness caused by starvation rendered him incapable of moving. With a certain definitiveness he sensed, terrified, that everything was about to collapse all around him, and so he waited. Not even the violin startled him when it fell from his mother's lap beneath her trembling fingers, giving off a note that echoed in the air.

"Dear parents," his sister said, striking the table by way of preamble, "things cannot go on like this. Even if you two perhaps do not realize it, I most certainly do. I am unwilling to utter my brother's name before this creature, and therefore will say only: we have to try to get rid of it. We have done everything humanly possible to care for it and show it tolerance, I don't think anyone would reproach us on this account."

"She is right a thousand times over," Gregor's father murmured under his breath. His mother, still incapable of breathing freely, began to cough dully into her lifted hand, a lunatic expression in her eyes.

Gregor's sister hurried over to her mother and held her forehead. Her words seemed to have given her father an idea, for he now sat up straight, playing with his uniform cap between the plates left behind on the table from the lodgers' supper and glancing over from time to time at a quiet Gregor.

"We have to try to get rid of it," his sister said,

addressing her words exclusively to Gregor's father this
time, for his mother was coughing too hard to hear
anything. "It'll be the death of you two, I can see it
now. When people have to work as hard as all of us have
been doing, it just isn't possible to endure these endless
torments at home. I cannot bear it anymore either."
And she burst into sobs, weeping so forcefully that her
tears flowed down upon her mother's face, from which
the girl wiped them with a mechanical gesture.

"Child," her father said sympathetically and with
noticeable compassion, "but what can we do?"

Gregor's sister just shrugged her shoulders as a sign
of the helplessness that had come over her while she
was weeping, in contrast to the confidence she'd dis-
played a moment before.

"If he understood us," Gregor's father said, half-
questioning; his sister, still caught up in her weeping,
shook one hand vehemently as a sign of how unthinkable she found this.

"If he understood us," his father repeated, closing his
eyes to absorb her conviction that this was utterly out
of the question, "then it might be possible to come to
an agreement with him. But as things stand—"

"It has to go," Gregor's sister cried out, "that's the

only way, Father. You just have to try to let go of the notion that this thing is Gregor. The real disaster is that we believed this for so long. But how could it be Gregor? If it were Gregor, it would have realized a long time ago that it just isn't possible for human beings to live beside such a creature, and it would have gone away on its own. We still would have been lacking a brother but we would have been able to go on living and honoring his memory. But now we have this beast tormenting us; it drives away our lodgers and apparently intends to take over the entire apartment and have us sleep in the gutter. Just look, Father," she suddenly shrieked, "he's starting again!" And in a fright that Gregor found bewildering, she now went so far as to leave her mother behind, launching herself from her chair as if she would rather sacrifice her mother than remain in Gregor's proximity, and ran to take cover behind her father who, agitated by the way she was carrying on, rose from his own chair and half-raised his arms as if to shield her.

But Gregor was far from wanting to frighten anyone, above all his sister. All he'd done was start to turn around to make his way back to his room, and admittedly this operation would have been hard not to notice, since in his current injured state he was obliged to use his head to help with this difficult maneuver; he kept raising it up and then thumping it against the floor. Pausing, he glanced around. His good intentions seemed to have been recognized; it had been only a momentary fright. Now all of them gazed at him sadly and in silence. His mother lay in her armchair, her extended legs pressed together, barely able to keep her eyes open in her exhaustion; his father and sister sat side by side, and his sister had draped one hand across her father's neck.

"Perhaps I'll be allowed to turn around now," Gregor thought and resumed his labors. He could not entirely suppress the wheezing this exertion produced, and now and then he had to rest. Otherwise no one was harassing him, he had been left to attend to matters on his own. When he had completed this rotation, he immediately made straight for the door to his room. He was astonished at how great a distance separated him from his destination, and he didn't understand how, weak as he was, he had been able to traverse the same distance just a little while before almost without noticing. Steadfastly concentrating only on crawling as quickly as possible, he scarcely paid any heed to the fact that not a word, not a cry came from his family to disturb him. Only when he was already in the doorway did he turn his head—not all the way around, as he felt his neck growing stiff, but even so he was able to see that all was unchanged behind him, except that his sister had risen to her feet. The last thing he saw was a glimpse of his mother, who had now fallen entirely asleep.

No sooner was he in his room again than the door was hastily pressed shut, locked and bolted. The sudden commotion at his back gave him such a frightful start that his little legs gave way beneath him. It was his sister who had hurried thus. She had already been standing there upright and waiting, then pounced so lightfootedly Gregor didn't hear her approach, and she cried out, "Finally!" to her parents as she turned the key in the lock.

"And now?" Gregor wondered, looking around in the dark. He soon made the discovery that he was no longer capable of moving at all. He wasn't surprised at this; on the contrary, it struck him as unnatural that he had actually until now been able to support himself on those thin little legs. As for the rest, he felt relatively at ease. Admittedly his entire body was racked with pain, but it seemed to him as if it was gradually becoming weaker and weaker and in the end would fade away altogether. Already he could scarcely feel the rotting apple in his back, nor the inflamed area surrounding it, both now enveloped in soft dust. He thought back on his family with tenderness and love. His opinion that he must by all means disappear was possibly even more emphatic than that of his sister. He remained in this state of empty, peaceful reflection until the clock-tower struck the third hour of morning. He watched as everything began to lighten outside his window. Then his head sank all the way to the floor without volition and from his nostrils his last breath faintly streamed.

When the charwoman arrived early the next morning, slamming the doors so loudly in her strength and haste—often as she'd been asked to avoid this—that sleep was out of the question anywhere in the apartment after her arrival, her usual cursory visit to Gregor's room revealed at first nothing out of the ordinary. She thought he was lying there so motionless on purpose, feigning indignation; she considered him perfectly capable of rational thought. Since she happened to be holding the long broom in her hand, she tried tickling Gregor with it from the doorway. When even this had no effect, she grew vexed and began to poke Gregor a little, and only when she had actually shifted him from the spot where he lay with no resistance at all were her suspicions roused. When soon thereafter the facts of the matter became clear to her, she gawked in surprise, gave a low whistle, then without further delay flung open the door of the bedroom and in a loud voice shouted into the darkness: "Come have a look, it's gone and croaked—just lying there, dead as a doornail!"

The Samsa couple shot upright in their marital bed and first had to struggle to recover from their shock at the charwoman's conduct before they were able to grasp her words. But then Herr and Frau Samsa hurriedly got out of bed, one on either side, Herr Samsa threw the blanket about his shoulders while Frau Samsa emerged wearing only her nightdress; in this state, they entered Gregor's room. Meanwhile the door to the living room, where Grete had been sleeping since the lodgers' arrival, had opened as well; she was fully dressed, as though she had not slept at all, as even the pallor of her cheeks seemed to prove. "Dead?" Frau Samsa asked, looking questioningly up at the charwoman, although she herself was free to investigate and, indeed, could see how things stood even without investigation. "I should say so," the charwoman said, and by way of proof, pushed Gregor's corpse quite some way to the side with her broom. Frau Samsa made a gesture as though she wanted to hold back the broom but didn't. "Well," Herr Samsa said, "now we can thank God." He crossed himself, and the three women followed his example. Grete, who did not take her eyes off the corpse for a moment, said: "Just look how skinny he was. He went such a long time without eating anything at all. All the food that went into his room would come out again just as before." And indeed Gregor's body was completely flat and dry, which hadn't really been noticeable until now when he was no longer raised up on those little legs and nothing else remained to distract the gaze.

"Grete, come sit with us for a bit," Frau Samsa said with a melancholy smile, and Grete, glancing back at the corpse, followed her parents into their bedroom. The charwoman shut the door and opened the window wide. Despite the early morning, the crisp air was already tempered by a certain mildness: after all, it was already the end of March.

The three lodgers now emerged from their room

and looked about in astonishment for their breakfast; they had been forgotten. "Where's breakfast?" the one in the middle asked the charwoman peevishly. But she just put a finger to her lips and then quickly, without a word, beckoned the lodgers into Gregor's room. They did as she bade them and with their hands in the pockets of their slightly threadbare little jackets, they surrounded Gregor's corpse in the room that had meanwhile become quite bright.

Then the bedroom door opened, and Herr Samsa appeared wearing his livery, with his wife on one arm, his daughter on the other. All three looked as if they'd been weeping; Grete kept pressing her face against her father's arm.

"Leave my home at once!" Herr Samsa said, pointing at the door without letting go of the womenfolk. "What do you mean?" the gentleman in the middle inquired, dumbfounded, and gave a saccharine smile. The two others held their hands at their backs and kept rubbing them together uninterruptedly, as if in gleeful expectation of a fight that was certain to be decided in their favor. "I mean exactly what I say," Herr Samsa replied, now advancing on the lodger flanked by his two companions. The lodger just stood there at first, looking at the ground, as if things were just rearranging themselves in his head into a new order. "So we'll be leaving," he said then, looking up at Herr Samsa as if this new humility that had suddenly come over him required him to petition for the approval of even this decision. Herr Samsa merely nodded curtly in his direction a few times, goggle-eyed. At this, the gentleman did, in fact, make haste to stride back out to the vestibule, where his two friends had been listening attentively for some moments, their hands at rest, and now they practically hopped and skipped in their hurry to follow, as if worried Herr Samsa might somehow precede them into the vestibule, cutting off their line of communication with their leader.

In the vestibule, all three of them took their hats from the coat rack, withdrew their walking sticks from the cane stand, made a silent bow and left the apartment. Displaying what soon proved to be an utterly unfounded mistrustfulness, Herr Samsa stepped out onto the landing with the two women; leaning against the banister, they watched as the three gentlemen descended the long staircase, moving slowly but at a steady pace and disappearing on each floor at a certain bend of the stairwell only to appear again a few moments later; the farther down they went, the more the Samsa family's interest in them faded, and when a butcher's apprentice came toward and then passed them on his way up, proudly bearing his tray upon his head, Herr Samsa and the women abandoned the banister, and all of them returned, seemingly relieved, to their apartment.

They decided to spend the day resting and to go out for a stroll; they had not only earned this respite from their work, but were desperately in need of it. And so they all sat down at the table and wrote three letters of excuse: Herr Samsa to his supervisor, Frau Samsa to her employer, and Grete to her superior. While they were writing, the charwoman came in to say she was leaving, as her morning's work was completed. The three scribes at first merely nodded without looking up, and only when the charwoman failed to go on her way did they glance up in annoyance. "Well?" Herr Samsa asked. The charwoman stood smiling in the doorway as if she had some splendid good fortune to announce to the family but would not do so until she was properly questioned. The nearly vertical little ostrich feathers on her hat, which had annoyed Herr Samsa for as long as she had been in the family's service, bobbed gently in all directions. "So what is it you want?" she was asked now by Frau Samsa, the member of the family for whom the charwoman still had the most respect. "Well," the charwoman replied, her own good-natured laughter making it impossible at first for her to go on speaking, "there's no need for you to go worrying about how to get rid of that mess in there. It's already taken care of." Frau Samsa and Grete bent down over their letters as if they meant to go on writing; Herr Samsa, who saw that the charwoman was about to start describing everything in detail, summarily silenced her with an outstretched hand. And since she was not permitted to say what she wished, she suddenly remembered the great hurry she was in, and so with an insulted air she cried, "So long, everyone," turned wildly on her heel, and with the most excruciating slamming of doors left the apartment.

"Tonight she'll be let go," Herr Samsa said, but received an answer neither from his wife nor his daughter, for the charwoman seemed to have disturbed the equanimity they had only just attained. They rose from their seats, went to the window, and remained there with their arms about each other. Herr Samsa turned in his chair to look at them and observed them quietly for a little while. Then he cried out: "So come here already. Let these old matters rest. And show a little consideration for me as well." At once the women obeyed, hurried over to him, caressed him and quickly finished their letters.

Then all three of them left the apartment together, something they had not done for months, and took the electric tram all the way to the open country-side at the edge of town. The car in which they sat all alone was entirely suffused with warm sunlight. Cozily leaning back in their seats, they discussed their future prospects, and on closer investigation it appeared that these prospects were not bad at all, for all three of their positions—something they had never before properly discussed—were in fact quite advantageous and above all offered promising oppor-tunities for advancement. The greatest immediate improvement in their situation, of course, would be easily achieved by moving to a new apartment; they now wished to take a smaller and cheaper but more convenient and above all more practical flat than their current one, which had been picked out for them by Gregor. As they were conversing in this way, Herr and Frau Samsa were struck almost as one while observing their daughter, who was growing ever more vivacious, by the thought that despite all the torments that had made her cheeks grow pale, she had recently blossomed into a beautiful, voluptuous girl. Growing quieter now and communicating with one another almost unconsciously by an exchange of glances, they thought about how it would soon be time to find her a good husband. And when they arrived at their destination, it seemed to them almost a confirmation of their new dreams and good intentions when their daughter swiftly sprang to her feet and stretched her young body.

AFTERWORD
THE DEATH OF A SALESMAN

Susan Bernofsky

Kafka's celebrated novella *The Metamorphosis* (*Die Verwandlung*) was written a century ago, in late 1912, during a period in which he was having difficulty making progress on his first novel. On November 17, 1912, Kafka wrote to his fiancée Felice Bauer that he was working on a story that "came to me in my misery lying in bed" and now was haunting him. He hoped to get it written down quickly—he hadn't yet realized how long it would be—as he felt it would turn out best if he could write it in just one or two long sittings. But there were many interruptions, and he complained to Felice several times that the delays were damaging the story. Three weeks later it was finished, on December 7, though it would be another three years before the story saw print.

As we know from Max Brod's diary, Kafka read his "bug piece" (*Wanzensache*) aloud to friends on November 24, 1912 (the first section), and again on December 15. People starting talking about it, and Kafka received a query from publisher Kurt Wolff in March 1913 on the recommendation of Kafka's friend Franz Werfel. Franz Blei, the literary editor of the new avant-garde journal *Die weißen Blätter*, expressed interest, and Robert Musil wrote as well, soliciting the novella for the more established *Die neue Rundschau*, though it was technically too long for the magazine's format. But months passed before Kafka had a clean manuscript ready for submission, and then World War I intervened, causing further delays (Musil was called up to serve, and because of the war Blei decided to stop printing literary texts). In the spring of 1915, René Schickele took over as editor-in-chief of *Die weißen Blätter*, and with Max Brod's help, Kafka placed the story there. It came out in October 1915, and then appeared in December 1915 (though dated 1916) as a slender volume published by Kurt Wolff Verlag in Leipzig.

The story's protagonist, Gregor Samsa, is the quintessential Kafka anti-hero. He has worked himself to the point of utter exhaustion to pay off his parents' debts, and his grotesque metamorphosis is the physical manifestation of his abasement. What exactly is he transformed into? In Kafka's correspondence with his publisher, he was adamant that the "insect" (*Insekt*) not be depicted on the jacket of the book. And although he and his friends used the word "bug" (*Wanze*) when referring casually to the story, the language that appears in the novella itself is carefully chosen to avoid specificity.

The epithet *ungeheueres Ungeziefer* in the opening sentence poses one of the greatest challenges to the translator. Both the adjective *ungeheuer* (meaning "monstrous" or "huge") and the noun *Ungeziefer* are negations—virtual nonentities—prefixed by *un*. *Ungeziefer* comes from the Middle High German *ungezibere*, a negation of the Old High German *zebar* (related to the Old English *tīber*), meaning "sacrifice" or "sacrificial animal." An *ungezibere*, then, is an unclean animal unfit for sacrifice, and *Ungeziefer* describes the class of nasty creepy-crawly things. The word in German suggests primarily six-legged critters, though it otherwise resembles the English word "vermin" (which refers primarily to rodents). *Ungeziefer* is also used informally as the equivalent of "bug," though the connotation is "dirty, nasty bug"— you wouldn't apply the word to cute, helpful creatures like ladybugs. In my translation, Gregor is transformed into "some sort of monstrous insect" with "some sort of" added to blur the borders of the somewhat too specific "insect"; I think Kafka wanted us to see Gregor's new body and condition with the same hazy focus with which Gregor himself discovers them.

That same blurred focus applies to other aspects of the story. Although Vladimir Nabokov—with his penchant for exactitude—has mapped out the Samsa flat in some detail, I am far from certain that Kafka himself— with his penchant for the blurred perceptions of bewilderment—was much concerned with the apartment's precise geography. How many rooms does this apartment have? Many, too many; just as Gregor, lying on his back in the story's opening sentences, discovers he has "these many little legs" waving in the air above him. Both are physical correlatives of a life that has gotten out of hand. Kafka is not even particularly attentive to the continuity of his cast of characters. Early on in the story we see the maid give notice and flee, only to find her still working in the household several pages later and in fact doing all the cooking, since now it is the cook who quit. Except for the charwoman who plays a starring role in the penultimate scenes, the household help is just part of the furniture of the story, like the cabinet that gets shifted to another room.

Even the main characters tend to appear categorically, named only by their functions: "father," "mother," "sister." Only one of them gets a name, Grete (rhymes with *beta*), but even she is usually referred to only as "sister" throughout, until the decisive moment near the end when she becomes instead a "daughter." By defining all these characters through their relationship to Gregor, Kafka slyly allows Gregor's point of view to dominate the story even when he is not actually present in the scene being described.

One leitmotif I was unable to preserve in translation is the theme of *ruhig/unruhig*. *Ruhig* denotes "calm," "peaceful," "quiet," "tranquil," "at ease," and *unruhig* its opposite. Starting with the *unruhigen Träumen* ("troubled dreams") in the first sentence, the narrative oscillates between untroubled and troubled, tranquil and harried, peaceful and unsettled. Since no one word in English fits well enough in all the contexts Kafka presents, I decided to translate the word in many different ways; but note when you are reading all these synonyms that you are watching a motif unfold.

The post-metamorphosis activity that gives Gregor

the greatest sense of freedom appears in my translation as "crawling": he enjoys crawling around the walls and ceiling of his room. Ironically, the German verb *kriechen* (which also translates as "to creep") has the additional meaning of "to cower." To *kriechen* before someone is to act sycophantically toward him. In this sense, too, Gregor's new physical state appears as a representation of his long-standing spiritual abjectness.

Finally Gregor has only himself to blame for the wretchedness of his situation, since he has willingly accepted wretchedness as it was thrust upon him. Like other of Kafka's doomed protagonists, he errs by failing to act, instead allowing himself to be acted upon. Gregor Samsa, giant bug, is a cartoon of the subaltern, a human being turned inside out. He has traded in his spine for an exoskeleton, but even this armorlike shell ("carapace" and "armor" are the same word in German, *Panzer*) is no defense once his suddenly powerful father starts pelting him with apples—an ironically biblical choice of weapon.

Gregor is a salesman, but what he's sold is himself: his own agency and dignity, making him a sellout through and through. For this reason I occasionally use the word "drummer" (commercial traveler) to describe his profession, referring back to another of his ilk, "a hardworking drummer who landed in the ash can like all the rest of them." That's Willy Loman as described by Arthur Miller in *Death of a Salesman* (1949). *The Metamorphosis* is Kafka's own *Death of a Salesman*, with all the sad, grubby tragedy, all the squalor. Like Willy Loman, Gregor is a suicide, though of a different sort: he dies a hunger artist, perishing of starvation because nothing tastes good to him anymore. And like Willy's, Gregor's death is the final service he performs for the benefit of his family.

At the same time Kafka's tragicomic tale—unlike Miller's—is very often hilariously funny. I imagine Kafka laughing uproariously when reading the story to his friends. Gregor's naïveté (one might also call it gullibility) combined with his earnestness and his tendency to sound somewhat overwrought in his assertions is perfectly risible. To bring out this side of the story, I've emphasized the slight tone of hysteria in Gregor's voice wherever it seemed justified.

The story is brutally comic in parts, and never more so than at the moment when it is revealed that—despite the fact that Gregor has been living more or less as an indentured servant to pay off his parents' ancient debts—in fact the family has plenty of money; not enough to allow them to stop working altogether, but a proper little nest egg. And although they are described as poor, they are never too hard up to retain the services of at least one domestic servant.

One last translation problem in the story is the title itself. Unlike the English "metamorphosis," the German word *Verwandlung* does not suggest a natural change of state associated with the animal kingdom such as the change from caterpillar to butterfly. Instead it is a word from fairy tales used to describe the transformation, say, of a girl's seven brothers into swans. But the word "metamorphosis" refers to this, too; its first definition in the *Oxford English Dictionary* is "The action or process of changing in form, shape, or substance; esp. transformation by supernatural means." This is the sense in which it's used, for instance, in translations of Ovid. As a title for this rich, complex story, it strikes me as the most luminous, suggestive choice.

Finally I would like to thank the friends and colleagues who helped me with suggestions and kind editorial interventions while I was working on this translation: Barbara Epler, Edith Grossman, Eliot Weinberger, Breon Mitchell, Christian Hawkey, Richard Gehr, Emily Bauman, Amanda Hong, and especially Sean Cotter, Glenn Kurtz, and Tim Watson. I would also like to thank Carol Bemis, Thea Goodrich, Ann Adelman, and Erach Screwvala.

New York, NY

August 2013